DEC 3 0 1993

KANKAKEE PUBLIC LIBRARY

W9-CBS-088

WITHDRAWN

# THE
# HIDDEN MESSAGE

PROPERTY OF
Kankakee Public Library

DEMCO

# Adventures
# of the Northwoods

# THE
# HIDDEN MESSAGE

## Lois Walfrid Johnson

**BETHANY HOUSE PUBLISHERS**

MINNEAPOLIS, MINNESOTA 55438

Big Gust Anderson, Mabel Ahlstrom, Harry Blue, Trader Carlson, Rev. Pickle, Charlie Saunders, and Peter Schyttner lived in the Grantsburg/Trade Lake area in the early 1900s. All other characters in this book are fictitious. Any resemblance to persons living or dead is coincidental.

Copyright © 1990
Lois Walfrid Johnson
All Rights Reserved

Published by Bethany House Publishers
A Ministry of Bethany Fellowship, Inc.
6820 Auto Club Road, Minneapolis, Minnesota 55438

Printed in the United States of America

---

**Library of Congress Cataloging-in-Publication Data**

Johnson, Lois Walfrid.
    The hidden message / Lois W. Johnson.
      p.  cm. — (The Adventures of the northwoods ; bk. 2)
    Summary: When their father leaves to earn money away from home. Kate and Anders assume more responsibility at the farm and uncover a mystery.

    [1. Swedish Americans—Fiction.  2. Mystery and detective stories. 4. Christian life—Fiction.]
I. Title.  II. Series: Johnson, Lois Walfrid. Adventures of the northwoods ; bk. 2.
PZ7.J63255Hi  1990
[Fic]—dc20                                     89–78390
ISBN 1–55661–101–3                                CIP
                                                             AC

To Jessica Lee,
Daniel Jeffrey,
and Nathaniel Kevin,
because I love you.

LOIS WALFRID JOHNSON is the author of over twenty books, including *You're Worth More Than You Think* and other books in the Let's-Talk-About-It Stories for Kids Series to help preteens make wise choices. Novels in the Adventures of the Northwoods Series have received awards from Excellence in Media, the Wisconsin State Historical Society, and the Council for Wisconsin Writers.

Lois and her husband, Roy, who plays a supportive role in her writing, live in rural Wisconsin. They are the parents of three married children.

# Contents

# 1

## Kate Listens In

*In* the darkness of a November night Katherine O'Connell woke suddenly. For a moment she lay without moving, wondering if something were wrong.

A sliver of moonlight slanted across the upstairs bedroom she shared with her sister Tina. The little girl still breathed evenly, her sleep peaceful. Kate slid farther beneath the quilt, trying to put aside her uneasiness.

Since moving to northwest Wisconsin, Kate had lost sleep more than once. Sometimes it was only a rooster that wakened her. Other times a screech owl shattered the peaceful woods around Windy Hill Farm. Then there was the night when Kate watched from the storeroom window and spied the disappearing stranger.

Now twelve-year-old Kate had no reason to stand watch, or so she thought. Closing her eyes, she tried to go back to sleep.

A moment later a murmur of voices brought Kate upright. Sliding out of bed, she reached for her robe and tiptoed across the cold wooden floor. Slowly, quietly, she turned the knob and opened the door just enough to slip through.

Still tiptoeing, Kate started down the stairs, keeping to the side of steps that squeaked. Mama and Papa's bedroom was on the first floor next to the dining room. Tonight, though, the voices came from the front room just beneath Kate and Tina's bedroom.

Four steps from the bottom, hidden by the wall between the stairs and the front room, Kate sat down. Pushing back her long hair, she leaned forward to listen.

"We need seed money for next year's crops." Papa Nordstrom's voice was low.

*Money!* thought Kate, disliking even the word. Kate's Irish father, Daddy O'Connell, had died in a construction accident. In the year that followed, Mama and Kate struggled to earn enough money for food and rent. Then Mama married Papa Nordstrom, and she and Kate moved from Minneapolis to Windy Hill Farm.

"He needs help with his three children," Mama had told her. "As we work together, I'll grow to love him."

Kate knew that had happened. Papa Nordstrom and Mama, Anders, Lars, Tina, and Kate had become a family.

But Kate hadn't expected to be the only one in the family and in her school who didn't speak Swedish. She hadn't expected to have to earn the respect of Anders, the new brother her age.

Now Papa Nordstrom spoke again. "Wages in the lumber camps are good this year."

For a moment there was silence. As she thought about his words, Kate felt an emptiness in her stomach. "I'm just getting to know you!" she wanted to cry out.

Papa Nordstrom's voice sounded sad. "I'd be gone two or three months during the worst part of winter."

Kate moved down another step, but couldn't hear Mama's answer.

"Yah" came Papa's Swedish yes. "Anders will help, and Lars, and Kate." His voice was gruff, the way it sounded when he cared deeply about something. "But I don't want to leave you."

"Can you think of any other way?" Mama asked softly.

For a time, Kate heard only the ticking clock. Then Mama spoke again. "If there isn't any other way, we'll do it. We'll handle it because we have to."

"But with the baby coming—" Papa said.

*A baby coming?* In her excitement Kate leaned farther forward, trying to hear more. Suddenly she tumbled down the remaining steps.

As she fell into the doorway of the front room, Papa Nordstrom jumped up. "Kate! Are you all right?"

Mama jumped up too, but her voice was stern. "I've told you, Kate, you aren't supposed to listen to other people's conversation."

"But, Mama, is it true you're going to have a baby?"

Mama's smile softened the sternness in her face. Standing up, she reached out and pulled Kate to her in a hug.

Mama was tall for a woman, and Kate short for her age. Kate also knew her own eyes were a deeper blue than Mama's. Yet now, as Kate looked up, Mama's eyes were shining.

"The baby will be born in the spring," Mama answered. "You're the first one to know."

The next morning at breakfast Mama and Papa Nordstrom told the other children the good news about the baby. But Anders and Lars and Tina also heard the sad news that Papa would go away to work in a lumber camp that winter.

"When you were at school yesterday, I butchered the pig," Papa told twelve-year-old Anders.

Anders nodded, his face solemn below his shock of blond hair. Like his father, his shoulders were muscular from farm work. But Papa had brown hair and a neatly trimmed moustache and beard.

Papa went on. "With this weather the pig should stay frozen. It's on the cookstove in the summer kitchen. The meat saw is there for you to cut off pieces when you need them."

Anders pushed his hair out of his eyes and nodded again. When days grew too warm for a fire in the house, the family cooked meals in the summer kitchen. In winter the small building wasn't heated.

As Papa turned to Lars, the nine-year-old looked just as serious as Anders.

"Lars, you and Anders split the wood and carry it in the way you always do. Take good care of the cows."

A tuft of hair stood up at the back of Lars's red head. Papa reached out, smoothed it down, and smiled. Lars blinked, then blinked again, as though holding back tears.

As five-year-old Tina slipped down from her chair, Papa set her on his lap. Tina's white-blond hair was pulled back in pigtails, and her blue eyes widened as Papa talked. "My little one, when the others are in school, you can help Mama all day long."

Then Papa looked at Kate and smiled gently. In that moment she remembered how he had helped her become part of his family. "Papa, I've been thinking. If I stopped taking organ lessons, could you stay home?" Even as Kate spoke, the words brought a pain within her. For years she'd wanted to take lessons and had only just begun.

Papa shook his head. "Playing the organ means too much to you, Kate. And even if you stopped, the money wouldn't be enough."

Then Kate saw the tears in Papa's eyes.

"Kate, my newest daughter, God will hold you with His special love."

Kate blinked as her own tears welled up. Surprised that he hadn't told her what work to do, she swallowed hard.

Clearing his throat, Papa turned back to the rest of the family. "If I bring a team of work horses, I'll earn more money. I'll take Dolly and Florie and get back sooner. You can put Wildfire to good use now, Anders."

As Papa mentioned the horse, Anders sat taller, pride shining in his face. But as he looked his father in the eyes, there was more. "We'll be all right, Papa. I'll take care of everything. Kate and Lars will help."

"All of you must be responsible," Papa continued. "Keep your head on your shoulders. Don't make Mama worry. Take good care of her and each other."

After praying for each one of them, Papa went out to the barn and harnessed the horses. Kate knew that when they came home from school, he'd be gone. A lonely ache crept into her heart.

It wasn't hard to remember what it was like after her first father, Daddy O'Connell, died. The rooms that Kate and Mama rented seemed silent and empty. Before, their lives had been filled with laughter. When Daddy came home from work, he often swung Kate off the floor with a big hug. Sometimes he danced around the kitchen, doing an Irish jig.

Now Kate wondered, *Will it feel just as empty with Papa Nordstrom gone?*

As Kate, Anders, and Lars started down the trail to Spirit Lake School, Kate turned to her oldest brother. "What will we do without Papa?"

"We'll make it," answered Anders. "We have to."

But Kate saw his eyes, and guessed how Anders felt. "I'll miss Papa," she said. She swallowed, quickly wiping away the tears that welled up.

Then she thought of all the things that could happen on a northwoods farm in 1906. *What if something goes wrong?*

# 2

## *The New Boy*

During the mile hike through the woods, Anders and Lars were strangely quiet. Anders led the way, his long legs stretching out. Lars followed, his freckled face and blue eyes solemn.

Scuffling her feet in the carpet of fallen leaves, Kate kept up with them. The November air was brisk, and she buttoned her wool coat against the cold.

Leaving Windy Hill Farm and Rice Lake behind, they walked along a ridge where the land fell sharply away on both sides. Soon they reached the steep hill overlooking Spirit Lake School.

At the bottom of the hill a creek flowed between them and the schoolhouse. Swollen by fall rains, the creek ran high between its banks. Lars jumped onto the log spanning the water.

Anders followed, moving so quickly that he seemed to run across. On the other side, he glanced up the hill toward school.

Instantly Anders stopped. "He's back."

"Who's back?" asked Kate as she stepped onto the log. Even now, after all the crossings she'd made, she felt almost as scared as on her first day at Spirit Lake School. The cold dark water rushed beneath her feet.

When Anders didn't answer, Kate asked again. "Who's back?"

"Stretch." Anders sounded as if he didn't like the idea. "Must have finished up harvesting."

As Kate reached the end of the log, she looked up the hill. Standing on the porch of the school was a thin boy with curly blond hair and a grin. To Kate's surprise he seemed even taller than Anders.

"Stretch?" she asked. "Why do you call him that?"

" 'Cause it fits."

"Because he's tall?"

"He's tall, all right," said Anders.

Kate realized he hadn't answered her question. "So that's why you call him Stretch?"

Anders looked grim, but wouldn't tell her more.

Finally Kate asked, "What's his real name? No one calls a baby Stretch."

Anders grinned. "Nope, they don't. They give 'em a name like Johnson or Peterson or Olson."

"What does that have to do with it?"

"Well, there's Big Gust Anderson."

Kate nodded. "The one in Grantsburg." The seven-and-a-half-foot-tall village marshal had helped Anders and Kate solve a mystery.

"And there's Church Barn Anderson and Bingo Anderson."

"Oh, you're teasing!" replied Kate.

Anders threw up his right hand. "I'm dead serious. There's so many Swede names the same that everyone calls 'em something different. There's Plaster Olson, Legs Olson, and Gloomy Gus Olson."

Lars chimed in. "And Dusty Olson and Stonewall Olson."

Kate started to laugh.

"Shoemaker Johnson, Tanner Johnson, Hitch Barn Johnson." Anders paused to draw a breath. "Happy Johnson, Spoon Hook Johnson, and Mule Johnson!"

Lars took up the chant. "Andrew Johnson One, Andrew Johnson Two."

"And Three and Four?" asked Kate.

Anders scratched his head. "I'm not sure. But there used to be a Johnson Number 22! And now we have the Johnson just called Stretch!"

"Do you call him Stretch to his face?"

"Yup," said Anders, heading up the hill toward school.

As the new boy went inside the building, Kate spoke softly. "He looks nice enough from here. What's the real reason you don't like him?"

When Anders didn't answer, Kate turned to Lars.

"He stretches the truth," the younger boy told her.

"What do you mean?"

At Anders' look Lars fell silent, but Kate wouldn't leave it alone.

"He's older than the rest of us," Anders said finally. "And he's *biiiiiig* trouble."

Kate laughed. "No one around here is big trouble!"

"Ha!" Anders sounded scornful. "That's what you think!"

"Then how come he's in school?" Kate asked. "Most boys stop coming around the end of eighth grade."

Though Kate prodded, Anders refused to say more. Finally she flipped her long black braid over her shoulders. "You're just making things up."

Anders turned to her, his eyes angry. "No, I'm not. And you stay away from him."

This time Kate giggled. "Who is he—the big bad wolf?"

Again Anders would not explain. "You listen to me."

"So?"

"So I know what I'm talking about."

Now Kate was angry. "You think you're boss just 'cause Papa's going away."

"If Papa was here, he'd tell you the same thing!" warned Anders darkly.

When Kate entered the schoolroom, most of the children were already at their desks. Their teacher, Miss Sundquist, stood near the back with the new boy. By comparison, she seemed small, and Kate knew Stretch must be close to six feet tall.

Just then he looked up over the teacher's head. Catching Kate's glance, he dropped one eyelid in a slow wink.

Quickly Kate turned away, embarrassed that she'd been caught watching. Reaching her desk, she put her books inside and took out her slate. As Miss Sundquist walked forward, Kate acted as if her only thought was on the lessons ahead.

But a moment later, Kate glanced over her shoulder. Stretch sat two desks back in the last seat of Kate's row and across the aisle from Anders. Though usually self-confident, Anders looked angry and uncomfortable.

Directly behind Kate was Erik Lundgren. Soon after Kate started Spirit Lake School, he had put her long black braid in his ink well. Like Anders, Erik was tall for his age. But unlike Anders' straight blond hair, Erik's was wavy and brown.

Kate hoped that Erik hadn't seen her look back at Stretch. Sometimes it seemed as if Erik saw everything.

" 'Mornin', Kate," he said now.

" 'Mornin', Erik," she replied in the same tone of voice.

"Ready for more ink on your dress?"

It was a constant battle between them. Whenever he threatened, she never quite knew whether he'd put her hair into his ink well again. Deep inside, she felt sure he hadn't meant to wreck her dress that day last March. Yet when she had swung her head, the end of her long braid had stained her dress with permanent ink.

Kate made a face at Erik and noticed that his hair was newly cut. "Got another bowl haircut?" she asked.

Erik flushed red, and Kate felt ashamed. Almost she wanted to say, "It doesn't really look that way." Almost she said it, but not quite. It might have seemed as though she were giving in to the war of words between them.

Erik and Anders were good friends, and both had strong arms and shoulders from farm work. Like Anders, Erik had a streak of kindness that told Kate he looked out for her, even during his endless teasing. But Erik cared more about his schoolwork than Anders did.

Kate looked across the aisle and smiled at Josie Swenson, the girl Kate knew best at Spirit Lake School. Slowly, gradually, she'd come to think of Josie as a friend.

"Kate, I've got to talk to you," Josie whispered. Her hazel eyes with their long dark lashes looked troubled.

"What's wrong?" asked Kate quickly, knowing it must be serious. What could be more important than a new boy in school?

"Something terrible," answered Josie, her voice low.

Kate leaned toward her. It took a lot to get Josie upset.

"Last night our steer was stolen." Josie looked as if she wanted to cry.

"Your steer?"

"The animal we've been raising for meat. We were going to butcher him any day now."

Josie's family lived on a farm near Spirit Lake School. The woods stretched between their place and Windy Hill, the farm where Kate lived.

"Stolen? You're sure?" Kate asked. She knew that sometimes animals worked their way outside the barbed wire fence. "Your steer didn't just wander away?"

Josie shook her head. "I don't know how Papa knows the difference. He won't talk about it in front of us. But for some reason, he's sure the steer was stolen."

"But nothing ever gets stolen around here." Kate hurt for Josie. "No one locks their doors. Everyone trusts everyone else."

"That's the worst of it." Josie fought back tears. "We never expected someone to steal. No one ever has before."

"Except when the disappearing stranger was around," Kate said.

"But he took small things," Josie replied. "Nothing as important as an animal."

In the morning sunlight the freckles across Josie's nose made her look younger than her twelve years. Yet Kate knew her friend often took care of eight younger brothers and sisters.

"It's your meat for all winter, isn't it?" Kate asked with a growing sense of loss for Josie.

Josie's nod was full of misery. "We don't have any other meat."

Then a gleam of hope entered her eyes. "Maybe you and Anders can solve this mystery too."

Before Kate and Josie could talk more, Miss Sundquist rang the small bell on her desk, asking for quiet. Usually calm and in control, the teacher seemed nervous. "As you see, we have a new boy with us," she announced. "I'm sure that most of you already know him."

Kate glanced back to see a careless grin cross Stretch's face. Again his bold glance met Kate's. Embarrassed, she quickly looked away.

# 3

## *Danger!*

*W*hen Kate reached home that afternoon, Papa was gone. Though he seldom talked unless something needed saying, his absence made the house seem quiet and lonely.

"I wonder how far he traveled yesterday," Kate said as she and Anders and Lars walked to school the next morning. "Do you think Papa was outside all night?"

"Nah," Anders told her. "He probably stopped at someone's house. He'd ask if he could sleep on the floor."

Then Kate thought about the horses and the cold night wind. "What about Dolly and Florie? Would someone put them in their barn?"

Anders shrugged his broad shoulders. "Don't know if they'd have room."

When Anders spoke again, his voice sounded different. "I don't like the way you look at him."

"Look at who?" Kate asked innocently.

"You know. Stop pretending."

"Don't know what you're talking about," insisted Kate.

Anders laughed, and the sound was harsh in the November woods. "I'm talking about Miss Katherine Nordstrom!"

"Katherine O'Connell, you mean!"

"Nordstrom."

"O'Connell." Since Kate's first day at Spirit Lake School, it had been an argument between them.

"And you know I'm talking about Stretch! You should see how you look." Anders crossed his eyes. A silly grin slid across his face.

Then the grin slipped away, and he sounded angry. "I mean it! I don't like the way you look at him!"

Kate felt the hot flush of embarrassment creep into her face. "Dumb boy! You're making up tales!"

"Am I?" asked Anders. "Then how come you're red? How come you're always watching what he does? He's up to no good, I tell you!"

"What do you mean?"

"He's just making eyes at Teacher."

"At Teacher?" Kate's voice was small.

"What do you think?" demanded Anders. "That's the only reason he's here. Last fall when we had an old lady teacher, he sure didn't show up after harvest."

"Miss Sundquist didn't teach last fall?"

"Nope!" said Anders. "She just finished three years of high school at Grantsburg. Started when the other teacher got sick and couldn't come back."

"But she's still older than Stretch," answered Kate. For a moment she hung on to a sliver of hope, wondering if Anders could be mistaken. Yet in the time she'd known him, Anders had seldom been wrong about anything.

Anders laughed. "Not much. Teacher's only a few years older than us."

Kate felt as if someone had punched her. *And I was dumb enough to think Stretch liked me.*

"If you want to like someone, like Erik Lundgren," Anders went on, as though reading her thoughts.

"Erik Lundgren?" scoffed Kate, flipping her long black braid over her shoulder. "Just because he's your friend?"

"Nope, because he's—"

"Responsible?" Kate laughed as she used Papa's word, but gave it a scornful twist.

This time it was Anders' turn to look uncomfortable.

Seeing his face, Kate pressed on. "He's responsible, all right. As Papa would say, 'Erik's got a head on his shoulders!' "

"Yup!" agreed Anders. "He does!"

"Wrecked my school dress last year putting my braid in the ink well."

"He didn't mean it," defended Anders.

"Well, whatever he meant, he wrecked my dress!"

But Anders refused to back down. "He just wanted to tease you."

Kate's laugh sounded even more scornful. "So?"

"So if you want to like someone, like Erik."

Kate stopped in the middle of the path. "I suppose next you're going to tell me I should like him 'cause he goes to our church."

Anders grinned. "Well, for a change you've got it figured out."

Kate stamped her foot. "I haven't got words to describe you!"

Anders acted as if he hadn't heard. "And if you weren't so brainless, you'd know that we choose who we like."

"Who says?" The idea startled Kate.

"Papa. And he's right. It can be a dumb choice or a good one. A stupid oaf like Stretch or someone who's—"

"Responsible," Kate finished for him. "Like Papa says, responsible. Then *you* better choose to like Josie." Kate's voice dripped with sugar.

When Kate saw the spark of anger in Anders' eyes, quickly replaced by his flush of embarrassment, she knew she'd struck home. "And you're just jealous of Stretch," she added for good measure. "Everyone else likes him. Why don't you?"

Wanting the last word, Kate stomped away.

She was still angry when they entered Spirit Lake School. In the cloakroom, she slammed her lunch pail down on a shelf. As she went to her desk, Kate made sure she didn't look toward Stretch.

"I have a warning for all of you," Miss Sundquist told the

class as they started the day. "Spirit Lake looks as if it's frozen, but the springs make it very treacherous. You must not go out on the ice."

After a few more announcements, she led the children in the pledge of allegiance. Then they said the morning prayer in unison: "Give me clean hands, clean words, and clean thoughts. Help me to stand for the hard right against the easy wrong."

Kate repeated the words with the other students. For the first time she wondered about them. *Help me to stand for the hard right against the easy wrong. What does that mean?* But she pushed the thought aside.

Arithmetic was always first, and Kate was never as quick at it as Anders and Erik. This morning she had more trouble than usual trying to concentrate. She kept wondering what was happening two desks back.

When it was time for morning recess, Kate stood up quickly to get her coat. As she went out on the porch of the school, she wrapped a scarf around her neck and pulled on mittens.

Stretch stopped beside her. "She don't know what she's talkin' about," he said softly.

Surprised, Kate looked up. Standing next to him, she felt even shorter than usual. Yet she also felt excited that Stretch wanted to talk with her. "Who doesn't know what?" she asked.

"Teacher. Says the ice ain't safe."

"If she says it, I believe it," Kate answered. "No reason to go down there anyway. Plenty to do on the playground."

"Playground?" Stretch's voice sounded scornful. "That's for babies."

Yet as he and Kate circled the frozen yard, the boys were choosing sides for a game. One of them called out. "Hey, Stretch! Come here!"

Someone else objected. "We get him! Com'on, Stretch! Be on *our* side!"

Taller and older than the other boys, Stretch would help any team win. But he shook his head and kept walking.

Kate followed him to the hill at the edge of the playground. There they stood above the road that passed the school. On the other side were trees, now bare of leaves. Beyond lay the shores of Spirit Lake.

"I tell you, I know I'm right." Stretch gazed toward the expanse of frozen water. "I was down there before school."

"Days have been warm," Kate reminded him.

"Nights have been cold," he answered. "Plenty cold."

In the morning sunlight the ice shone. To Kate it looked inviting. "We can ice skate soon."

"We can skate *now*. Com'on and see."

"Teacher said no," protested Kate.

"She just said that 'cause some school-board member told her."

Stretch started down the hill. At the bottom he looked back. "What're you scared of?"

For a moment Kate stood there, feeling uneasy. But then a new thought came to her. *Maybe it isn't Teacher he likes, after all.* Step by step, Kate edged down the hill. "There's not much time."

"If we hurry, we'll get back," Stretch answered.

Kate still didn't feel right about it, but she pushed her uneasiness aside. *If I don't go, he'll think I'm a sissy.* Besides, it'd be fun walking to the lake with Stretch.

"We don't have to go out on the ice," he told her. "Let's just look." In spite of his lazy manner, Stretch walked quickly.

As Kate kept up, she asked, "Did you hear about Josie's steer?"

"What about it?"

"That it was stolen?"

"That so? Well, a steer's only a steer."

"No, it's not! They fattened him for two years to have him ready for winter." For a moment Kate wondered how Stretch could be so cold and heartless. She still felt bad for her friend. "Josie's got eight brothers and sisters!"

"Why do they think the steer was stolen?" Stretch asked.

Kate felt relieved that he sounded more concerned about the whole thing. Just the same, she could only tell him, "I don't know. Josie's father doesn't say *why*. But he *thinks* it was stolen."

Within a few minutes they reached a spot where the road ran close to the lake. As Stretch slid down the steep bank, Kate followed.

The ice had frozen smooth and clear. Kate looked across the

lake to the morning sun. Yet the sunlight did not warm her. Shivering, she tightened the scarf around her neck and felt glad for her wool coat and mittens.

As she squinted against the light, Kate saw a dog far out on the ice. The brown, black, and white hair seemed familiar. Suddenly Kate recognized him. "That's Lutfisk!"

"*Lute fisk?*" Stretch drawled out the word for the dried cod that Swedes soak in lye and eat at Christmas.

"Anders' dog. When he was a puppy, he got into the lutfisk and gobbled it up before Anders caught him. Must have followed us to school."

"Nice dog," said Stretch.

"Yup," answered Kate, then realized she sounded like Anders. "But he shouldn't be out on the ice. I'll get Anders to call him."

"No need." Stretch sounded helpful. "I'll get the dog for you." He called, but Lutfisk did not respond.

"Come here, Lutfisk!" Kate shouted.

In the crisp morning air the dog turned his head. Yet when Kate called again, Lutfisk did not start toward them.

"He hears me," said Kate. "What's the matter with him?" Stepping onto the ice, she moved closer to the dog.

"Come on, Lutfisk!" she tried once more. The dog lifted his head.

Then she remembered Anders' signal for sending Lutfisk after the cows. Raising her arm high, she motioned to the right. Even so, Lutfisk did not respond.

Kate turned to Stretch, who stood on the nearby shore. "You try."

Stretch's shout seemed to echo in the cold air. There was no doubt that the dog heard. Yet as he started toward them, Lutfisk barked, then stopped.

"Come on, boy!" urged Kate, edging still farther onto the ice.

Stretch called again, but instead of obeying, Lutfisk lowered his head and growled.

In the next instant Kate heard a loud crack. She went cold with fear.

The ice cracked again, louder this time. Quickly Kate stepped back. But her movement made things worse.

Once more the ice cracked. Suddenly it opened beneath her.

# 4

## *Fight for Life*

$\mathcal{A}$s Kate plunged through the opening in the ice, she heard Lutfisk bark. Then she slipped deep beneath the surface of the lake.

Gasping, she choked on a mouthful of water. The cold seized her body, sending pain through her stomach and chest.

"You can swim," she told herself as she felt the shock. "You can swim."

Yet her clothing and shoes were heavy weights, pulling her down. Kate tried to lift her arms, and her coat sleeves filled with water. She stretched down a foot and could not touch bottom.

Panic washed over her, and she fought for air. She kicked, then kicked again. Surfacing, she took a deep breath and cried out, "Help! Help!"

Hair streamed in her eyes, clouding her vision. She heard only the barking of the dog.

*Where's Stretch?* Frantically, Kate looked toward shore, but saw no one.

The edge of the hole was not far away, and Kate reached for the ice with mittened hands. Her long scarf got in the way. Pulling it from her neck, she let it go, and fought for the edge of the hole.

As she touched the ice, it broke off. Her arms thrashed the water, breaking a wider circle. The weight of her coat pulled her down, below the surface.

Once more the sunlight disappeared, and black water closed around her.

Gasping for breath, Kate kicked, but saw only darkness. She kicked again. *Where's the hole?*

Her legs were numb now, and she wasn't sure if they moved. Her ears pounded. She seemed to spin in the black water.

Filled with panic, Kate fought her way upward. Then her head bumped something. *I'm under ice!* The terror of it over-whelmed her as she struggled to see light. Off to one side—maybe.

Stretching out her arms, she tried to head in that direction. Suddenly she found open water and surfaced. As she gasped for air, her head stopped spinning.

This time she heard a voice.

"Kate! Kate!"

*Stretch?* The voice seemed far away, but she listened.

"Take off your coat!"

Kate reached for the buttons. But her mittens got in the way. She forgot to kick and started to sink.

"Forget the coat!"

Kate heard the voice, but felt numb. *I'm so cold.*

"This way! Reach out your hands."

*My hands? Where are my hands?*

"Touch the ice with your mittens!"

Kate stretched out her arms, but wasn't sure if anything happened.

"You're almost there."

Through her panic Kate saw the edge of the hole about a foot away. Yet that foot seemed like a mile.

With her last ounce of strength, Kate reached again. Her mittens touched the edge, but the ice broke away. Again she felt herself sink.

"Com'on, Kate!"

Numbly, Kate kicked, unsure if her legs moved. The ice broke again.

"One more try," called the voice. "Almost got it."

But Kate's legs would no longer move. She lifted her arms, trying to reach out, and knew that she couldn't.

"Help her, God. Help her!"

Even though her mind seemed frozen, Kate heard fear in the voice.

"Try again!" The voice was steadier now, and the sound of panic gone.

This time Kate's mittens clutched the ice, and it did not break.

"Hold them there!" the voice shouted.

Kate's teeth chattered. It took all of her breath to speak. "I can't."

"Let 'em freeze to the ice!"

Kate's shoulders ached, and time stretched out forever. But then she knew the voice was right. Her mittens froze, holding her there.

"Don't move! I'll be right back."

"Don't go!" Kate gasped out.

But no answer came, and Kate knew he was gone. She trembled with fear. *I'm going down!* But the mittens held her.

*I'm so tired.*

Then the voice was back. Though far away, it sounded familiar. Was it Stretch?

"I've got a branch," the voice said. "See it? Right next to your hands?"

Dimly Kate saw the branch. A long thick one.

"Take one hand out of your mitten. Hang on to the branch. Got it?"

Kate's hand trembled, but her fingers curled around the end of the branch.

"Take your other hand. Hang on. Keep your legs straight. I'll pull you out."

The branch began to move, and Kate clung to it. Yet as her body started to slide, the ice broke away. Once again she found herself slipping farther into the water.

"Don't let go!" the voice warned. "Hang on!"

Her hands numb, Kate wondered if she could. But she still heard the voice cry, "Hang on! I'll try again!"

A second time the ice broke. On the third try, Kate's arms, then her stomach, legs, and feet slid onto the ice.

It held.

Kate felt herself being dragged. Then whoever pulled the branch stopped. Someone slapped her cheeks. From far away, a voice called, "Kate!"

Her eyelids felt weighted, but she opened them.

"You're safe," said the voice.

Kate looked up, expecting to see Stretch. Instead, Erik's face hovered above hers. Even through the fog, Kate saw that his eyes looked scared.

Kate shivered and tried to speak. She wanted to tell him she was sorry for saying he had a bowl haircut. She wanted to apologize for every awful thing she'd ever said. But no words came.

Erik didn't seem to care. "You're all right now, Kate."

She closed her eyes as he went on. "You have to walk. You have to get where it's warm."

"I can't," Kate answered, then felt surprised that her voice worked. Her teeth chattered. "I can't feel my feet."

"I'll help."

Taking her hands, Erik pulled her up. "Hang on to my neck." He raised Kate's arm, and the sleeve crackled in the cold.

Kate looked at it dumbly, wondering what was wrong. But Erik slid under her arm and started walking.

Half pulling, half carrying her, Erik climbed the steep bank near the lake. When Kate slipped, he slid under her arm once again. By the time they reached the road, her long braid had turned to ice. Her body trembled with cold inside her stiff coat.

They started toward school, Erik tugging, Kate staggering. Partway there, Kate saw Anders and Lutfisk running toward them. Her brother's face looked white.

"What happened?" he demanded in a voice Kate had never heard before. "Lutfisk came after me."

Reaching Kate's side, Anders stretched out his hands. By crossing their arms, the boys made a chair to carry Kate.

On the way back to school, Erik explained. "I heard Lutfisk bark."

"You went down to the lake?" Anders asked Kate, his voice

angry. "After Teacher said not to?"

Kate's teeth chattered so hard she could not speak.

"How dumb can you get?" Anders exclaimed. "You could have drowned!"

Tears came to Kate's eyes. She sagged, but Erik held her up. "Be quiet, Anders!" Erik snapped roughly.

Kate heard something in his voice, something she didn't understand. For now she just felt glad that Anders said no more.

As they came to the schoolyard, Kate saw a horse and buggy. *Why was it there?* It didn't make sense. Yet Kate couldn't think beyond her shivering.

Anders recognized the horse. "Miss Ahlstrom's here!"

In spite of her misery, Kate sensed the warning. "Who's Miss Ahlstrom?" she asked through chattering teeth.

"The superintendent of schools," answered Erik, his voice soothing.

"For the whole county," Anders added grimly. "She visits all the schools. Comes to make sure the teacher's doing everything right."

Kate's shoulders started to shake, both from dread and cold.

But Anders went on. "You're in big trouble now!"

As Kate's arms and hands trembled, tears slid down her icy cheeks. Yet she felt too weak to wipe them away.

"Be quiet, Anders!" Erik said again. "Let her be."

Their arms still crossed in a makeshift chair, the boys carried Kate up the steps of the school.

When they walked into the entryway, Miss Sundquist was standing in front of the class. As she looked toward Kate, the teacher stopped midsentence.

Every child looked back.

"Study your lessons," ordered Miss Sundquist, heading toward Kate and the boys.

As Erik and Anders set Kate down, her knees felt weak. She started to slip to the floor, but Erik hung on and kept her from falling.

Instead of the stern words Kate expected, Miss Sundquist spoke softly. "Come here," she said, drawing Kate into the cloakroom. "What happened? You're turning blue."

Moving quickly, the teacher grabbed towels from a high shelf. Taking her own coat from a hook, she put it down on a bench next to Kate. "You must change at once," Miss Sundquist said. Then she went out, shutting the door behind her.

Kate's fingers trembled as she pulled off her icy clothes. The teacher's coat was long, and Kate buttoned it from top to bottom.

When Miss Sundquist returned, she had a pair of wool stockings for Kate's blue-with-cold feet. "We'll dry your dress and coat by the stove," the teacher said as she helped Kate up. "Now come and sit as close to the heat as you can without burning yourself."

As Kate left the cloakroom, every child again turned to stare at her. But Kate was still so cold and miserable she didn't care. Making her way to the wood stove, she huddled close.

It was a long time before Kate stopped shivering.

In front of the class Miss Sundquist was again stern. "I believe you all know how serious this is. Kate is still so weak, I'll talk to her later. Starting tomorrow night, she'll stay after school the rest of this week. Now, can someone tell me why she went down to the lake?"

As the teacher looked around the room, everyone remained silent.

For the first time, Kate saw a lady sitting in a corner near the back. Her large hat had an even larger plume that curled down over the side of her face. In spite of her dread that this must be Miss Ahlstrom, Kate felt surprised by the young woman's beauty.

As Miss Sundquist waited for an answer, Kate saw Stretch in his usual seat, the last in his row. For an instant their gaze met. Then Stretch looked down.

Seeing him there in warm dry clothes, Kate felt angry. *Where did you go when I fell through the ice?*

"Someone must know something," said Miss Sundquist when no one spoke up. "Erik? Anders? What happened?"

Anders looked at Erik.

Erik looked uncomfortable, but he was the one who answered. "I heard Lutfisk barking."

"*Lute fisk?*" asked Miss Sundquist, as though unsure she'd heard the name correctly.

"Anders' dog. Must have followed him to school today. When I first saw Lutfisk, he was out on the ice. Kate was in the water, waving her arms."

"And you, Anders?"

"Lutfisk came and got me, then ran toward the lake. I went after him and saw Erik bringing Kate back to school."

"So, Erik. You rescued Kate from the water? Will you tell us how you did that?"

Quietly Erik described what had happened.

When he finished, tears glistened in Miss Sundquist's eyes. "I believe you all realize that Kate would have drowned if Erik hadn't helped her."

From her place near the stove, Kate watched Erik. He looked down, embarrassed by Miss Sundquist's praise.

But the teacher went on. "Erik, I especially want to thank you for keeping your head. If you hadn't, you also would have gone through the ice. Both of you could have drowned."

The room was silent then, and Kate felt uncomfortable. In that long quiet moment, she looked toward the back of the room.

Throughout the explanation, Stretch hadn't spoken a word. And Erik never mentioned him.

Again Kate felt angry with Stretch, so angry that she wanted to cry out, "Because of you, I could have died!"

# 5

---

# *Sounds in the Night*

$\mathcal{S}$tretch still avoided Kate's eyes.

By now Kate was warm enough to realize the seriousness of what she'd done. Besides nearly drowning, there was something else.

As she glanced back toward Miss Ahlstrom, Kate remembered what Anders said. "She comes to make sure Teacher's doing everything right." Kate liked Miss Sundquist and didn't want to spoil things for her.

In that moment Miss Ahlstrom stood up and walked forward. When she reached the front of the class, she turned toward where Kate huddled by the wood stove. "Kate, I trust you'll be wise enough not to go out on unsafe ice again."

Kate's cheeks burned with embarrassment.

Miss Ahlstrom went on. "I trust you'll value your life more from now on."

Kate wanted to ask, *What do you mean by that?*

But already the county superintendent had turned back to the rest of the class. "I also trust that all of you have learned a lesson," Miss Ahlstrom said. Then her voice softened. "Erik, I want to thank you for your heroism. It is seldom that a boy your age thinks and acts so quickly."

Miss Ahlstrom turned to the teacher. "Miss Sundquist, I value your fine handling of an emergency situation."

Kate breathed a sigh of relief.

Soon after, Miss Ahlstrom left the school. As her horse and buggy passed outside the window, the wheels creaked on the frozen dirt road.

Most of the day Kate stayed near the stove, warming up and drying her clothes and shoes. More than once she stared at Stretch, daring him to look her in the eye. *Where were you when I needed help?* she thought. Yet she never caught him looking her way.

By the time school was over, Kate's dress was dry, and she put it back on. Her coat was still wet and her shoes soggy. But Josie and Miss Sundquist loaned her their sweaters. Kate wore one on top of the other and carried her coat over her arm.

As she and Anders and Lars started home, Anders spoke up. "Of all the things you could possibly do, that was the stupidest!"

Kate lowered her head and looked at the ground.

"Papa tells us to be responsible, and there you go, out on the ice," Anders went on. "What were you thinking of?"

"I saw Lutfisk," Kate spit out, unable to remain silent. "I was afraid he'd fall through."

"You could have called him. One whistle, and he'd have come off the ice."

"I thought he'd come. He's obeyed me before, and you know it!"

"That's what's hard for me to figure out," Anders said. "Why didn't he now?"

Through the panic of those terrible moments in the water, Kate thought back. Why hadn't Lutfisk come? There was something she needed to remember, something that happened.

Then a picture flashed into her mind. *That's it!* she thought excitedly. Just before the ice broke, she heard Lutfisk growl a warning. Was it because he sensed Kate's danger on the lake? Or was it something else?

Now she felt afraid to ask. *I can't tell Anders I went down there with Stretch. I can't tell him that Stretch said the lake was safe, and I forgot and went out on it.*

Kate dreaded what Anders would say if he found out. Even worse, she still had more to face.

Anders reminded her now. "I hate to think what Mama's going to say when she hears you fell through the ice."

" 'Specially when Papa said we're s'posed to help her," added Lars, his eyes solemn.

Kate knew they were right. The empty feeling in her stomach tightened in a knot of fear. Her wet shoes and cold feet added to her misery.

*What can I do?* she asked herself for the hundredth time. As she wondered what Mama would think, the tightness in her stomach moved into her throat. Kate felt like choking.

In that moment she made up her mind. "I'm not going to tell Mama."

"You're not going to tell her?" Lars looked shocked.

"I won't give her the letter from Teacher."

"But that would be lying!" exclaimed Lars.

Anders also looked disturbed. "You don't have any choice, Kate. You have to tell her."

"Why?" asked Kate boldly.

"Why?" Lars's eyes reminded Kate of a hurt puppy. A hurt, yet also angry puppy. For a moment he seemed to search his mind for an answer. "Because it's honest," he finished with an air of triumph.

"Honesty, fiddlesticks!" Kate flipped her black braid over her shoulder. "It's not that I'm lying to Mama. I just won't tell her. That's different."

"No, it's not," argued Lars, sounding sure of himself.

But when Kate stared back at him with her chin up, he looked away, as though not liking what he saw.

"You can't get by with it," warned Anders.

"Miss Sundquist won't see Mama for a while," answered Kate, her voice resentful. "By the time she does, she'll have forgotten."

"Someone else will tell Mama," said Lars.

"Who?" asked Kate. "Are you a tattletale?" She sounded like a cat ready to pounce.

Quickly Lars shook his head, but again he looked away as though he'd seen a stranger.

"And you?" Kate turned to Anders. "Are *you* a tattletale?"

"Aw, come on, Kate. You know I'm not. But Mama will hear from a neighbor or someone . . ." His voice trailed off.

Kate wondered if she and Anders were thinking the same thing. With winter coming, Mama could be pretty much alone on the farm.

"It might work," Anders said slowly as though not liking the sound of his words.

"It might, but it shouldn't," Lars stated stoutly. "Papa says we should be honest, no matter what it costs."

"Papa says this, and Papa says that!" exclaimed Kate angrily. "You tell on me, and when you do something wrong, I'll tell on you!"

Lars stepped back as though she'd slapped him.

Instantly Kate knew she had hurt him. She'd hurt something that had always been special between them.

The next moment Kate remembered how Lars helped her when she first came to northwest Wisconsin. She knew she should say she was sorry, but the words stuck in her throat.

Then the moment was gone. Without looking back, Lars took off, running to the farmhouse.

"Do you think he'll tell?" Kate asked.

Anders shook his head. "But you've started something." His voice was grim. "Something you're going to be sorry for."

When they reached the house, Kate avoided going into the kitchen as she usually did. Instead, she slipped through the front door and up the steps to her room. Quickly she changed out of the borrowed clothing into her everyday work dress.

"Now what can I do?" she asked herself.

The farmhouse had two stoves that used wood—a cookstove in the kitchen and another for heating in the dining room. In winter the family used both stoves for drying wet clothes. But Kate didn't dare hang her coat near either one of them. Mama would wonder why it was wet.

Spreading it out, Kate pulled the coat over the floor grate that let in heat from the dining room. Then she hurried down the steps into the kitchen.

Lars sat at the table drinking milk and eating oatmeal cookies. Mama stood peeling potatoes for supper.

"I can do that, Mama," Kate offered quickly. "Sit down and rest."

Mama looked grateful. "Thanks, Kate. You're always such a good girl."

Kate smiled, but felt uncomfortable. As she looked beyond Mama, she saw Lars. He held up two fingers making horns behind his head.

Kate turned her back on Lars. Bending over the potatoes, she peeled them as though she didn't have another thought in the world. But she was really figuring out what to tell Mama.

After a time Kate spoke up. "I'll be late every night the rest of the week. I'm going to help Miss Sundquist after school."

Then Kate saw Lars's face. He looked shocked. Behind Mama's back, he stared at Kate and mouthed the words, "Big liar!"

Kate glanced away, but couldn't push her uneasiness aside. It was the first time she could remember telling Mama something that sounded true but wasn't. *I'm not really lying*, Kate told herself. *I'm just not telling why I'll help Teacher.*

"It's nice you want to help," answered Mama. "But what about your schoolwork?"

"I'll do it at night," Kate quickly assured her.

"And your organ practice?"

"At night, Mama," Kate said again.

*And I'll knit mittens, too, and a scarf*, Kate added to herself. *I'll light a candle and knit them in my room so Mama doesn't find out mine are down in the lake.*

Aloud Kate said, "Don't worry, Mama. I'll get everything done."

All through supper and early evening Kate helped in every way she could. After Mama went to bed, Kate slipped downstairs and hung her coat over a chair to dry. She moved the chair as close to the stove in the dining room as she dared. Nearby she set her still-wet shoes.

The minute she crawled into bed, Kate fell asleep.

In the middle of the night she woke up. For a long moment she lay half awake, half asleep, listening. This time she heard no murmur of voices from the room below. It was something else. Something that seemed like bad dream.

Then Kate guessed what must have wakened her. More than any other sound she knew, it filled her with panic.

Sharp teeth chewing wood in the walls! *Gnaw. Gnaw. Gnaw!*

Kate's fingers tightened into nervous fists. Then she heard the scamper of little feet across the wood floor. *A mouse in my bedroom!*

Clutching the quilt, Kate pulled it over her head. For a long time she lay there, her heart pounding.

"Wake up, Tina!" she whispered. Tina had lived on the farm all her life. Maybe she wouldn't be scared. But the five-year-old slept on, and Kate felt embarrassed to poke the little girl.

After a long time, Kate pushed back the quilt and listened. At first she heard nothing and thought the mouse had gone. Then the gnawing started again.

Kate drew up the quilt so fast that it pulled out at the bottom. *He'll get my feet!*

Kate crept to the bottom of the bed, still hiding beneath the quilt. Leaning over, she struggled to tuck it in. From inside the quilt she couldn't manage. But in the darkness of the room she felt too afraid to stand on the floor and put it back where it belonged.

Finally Kate gave up and lay down again. Curling up in a ball, she made sure both her head and feet were covered.

"What should I do?" she almost cried out. Her terror seemed to grow with every minute. "If I tell Mama, she might ask me to set a trap."

Kate had seen the mousetrap Papa Nordstrom used. A little wooden box, it had a small grate to help a mouse sniff out the cheese inside. To reach that cheese, a mouse went up a ramp and through a hole. When it passed through a second hole, a spring dropped down, and the mouse couldn't escape.

Kate wasn't sure what would be worse—not catching the mouse or catching it. She might have to empty the trap. She'd have to carry the box outside. She'd have to open the lid on top and let the mouse go.

From her hiding place under the quilt, Kate shuddered. In the whole world she could not think of anything worse. What if she had to ask Anders or Lars to empty the trap? They'd know. Lars had been there once when she saw Papa find a mouse. What if Lars guessed how scared she felt?

Kate trembled, thinking about it. *He and Anders would laugh at me. And what else would they do?*

# 6

## *Wildfire*

*At* school the next morning Kate heard Anders and Erik talking.

"You're renting the farm next to us?" Anders asked. From the expression on his face, it was the best news he'd heard in a long time. "When will you move?"

"Two days from now," Erik answered. "The house is empty. We want to get in before winter."

Secretly Kate felt glad. Sometimes when she glanced Erik's way, she found him watching her. Now and then she wondered why he seemed so interested in what she did. But whenever Erik had a chance to tease her, he seemed like his old self.

When Miss Sundquist called her to the front, Kate dragged herself to her feet. Her leather shoes felt stiff and uncomfortable from drying next to the wood stove. They also squeaked from being wet.

Slowly Kate walked forward. In the quiet room her shoes sounded loud. *Squeak. Squeak. Squeak.*

Erik was the first to notice. As Kate glanced back, she saw him grin. Then Erik snickered, and the boy across the aisle looked up. By the time Kate reached the front, she heard muffled giggles from around the room.

Kate's cheeks burned hot. Quickly she sat down on the bench near Miss Sundquist's desk. As she read for the teacher, Kate thought of one thing. *What will happen when I walk back?*

The other children seemed to wait for that moment. When Kate stood up, every student looked her direction.

Hoping her shoes wouldn't squeak, Kate kept her knees straight. With her feet flat, she walked stiff-legged.

But then she heard Erik whisper. "Hey, scarecrow! What's the matter with your knees?"

As Kate bent her feet, her shoes creaked ominously. *Squeak. Squeak. Squeak.*

Between each creak came snickers from every corner.

Reaching her desk, Kate sat down quickly, took out a book, and pretended she was reading. Even when Erik poked her, she refused to look up.

———

Two days later, on Thursday, Erik stayed home from school to help his family move. Late that afternoon Kate and Anders started across the field between their home and Erik's. Mama had packed baskets of food.

As they reached the woods between the two farms, the dusk of the November day settled in. When Anders stopped to light the lantern, Kate felt glad.

The farmhouse Lundgrens rented had two rooms downstairs and a loft overhead. Erik and his older brother John would sleep in the loft. Their younger sister Chrissy had a cot in the kitchen, and Erik's papa and mama a bed in the front room.

John had finished eighth grade and now worked at home with his father. But the next morning Erik and Chrissy met Anders, Kate, and Lars at a fork in the trail. From there they walked to school.

As always, Erik and Anders had a good time. As they went ahead, Kate watched them laugh together. In spite of the way Erik teased about her squeaky shoes, Kate still wanted to talk to him. There were gaps in the story he told Miss Sundquist, gaps only Kate knew about. Yet she didn't want to ask those questions in front of Anders.

Friday marked the last endless day of staying after school. On Saturday morning Kate tucked her books under her arm and set out for her organ lesson. Leaving the house, she started down the wagon track with Lutfisk following.

As she came to the barn, she saw Anders hitching his horse Wildfire to the farm wagon. "Hop in!" he called as he finished. "My turn to do the creamery run. I'll take you partway."

A black mare with a white star and four white socks, Wildfire was long-legged and spirited. She was saddle broke when Anders bought her after the Burnett County Fair. In the time since, he had often hitched the mare to a farm wagon, getting her used to that.

"First time I've taken a passenger," Anders said as Kate climbed into the wagon. "Hold the reins while I untie her."

"You're sure she's ready?" asked Kate, not convinced that she wanted a ride behind a skittish horse. Still, it was a four-mile walk to their church at Four Corners, a settlement south of Trade Lake.

"Yup, she's ready," Anders told her as Kate took the reins. "Just hold her steady while I get in."

Once seated, Anders flicked the reins lightly across Wildfire's back.

As they left the farmyard, Mama called to them. "Be sure to stop at Trader Carlson's, Kate!"

Kate nodded and waved, while Anders urged the horse to move out. The mare turned her ears to the sound of his voice and started down the wagon track to the main road. Lutfisk bounded ahead.

"Wildfire's doing great!" Kate exclaimed.

Anders nodded proudly. "Took a while to get her used to a wagon. But she's steady now."

Just then Anders noticed Lutfisk streaking for the woods. Anders let out a long sharp whistle that pierced the stillness of the November day. Instantly Lutfisk stopped.

Turning, the dog picked up speed as he ran back to Kate and Anders. When Lutfisk reached the wagon, he was panting, and his long tongue hung out.

Kate laughed. "He wags his tail so hard, the back of his body swings with it!"

For a moment she watched Lutfisk follow alongside the wagon. "Wish he'd obey me the way he does you." There was something Kate still wanted to find out, but she had to be careful how she asked. "You know the day I fell through the ice?"

"Yup?" answered Anders.

"When I called, Lutfisk lifted his head and looked my way. Then he barked."

"But he didn't come, you said. That's strange."

"Strange, all right," said Kate. "What's more, he growled."

"Lutfisk growled at *you*?" Anders looked at her in disbelief.

"He hadn't growled at me since my first day on the farm."

"Strange," muttered Anders again. "Really strange." Then he shot a quick look at Kate. "Sure you're telling me everything?"

Suddenly Kate felt uncomfortable. In that instant she guessed what had happened. But she wasn't willing to tell Anders that Stretch stood next to her. *Maybe that's why Lutfisk growled. He doesn't trust Stretch.*

"Will you show me how to whistle through my teeth?" she asked instead.

Anders laughed. "Girls don't whistle that way."

"Why not?"

His blue eyes turned serious. "It isn't ladylike."

Kate wasn't sure if Anders was teasing or not. "If I whistled like you, Lutfisk would always come."

"Maybe. Maybe not."

"He would," said Kate, determined now that Anders teach her. "What do you do? How do you make such a loud sound?"

Anders drew his lips tight and blew. His long sharp whistle pierced the air. Lutfisk pricked up his ears and came close to Anders' side of the wagon.

Kate tried to imitate Anders, but no sound came.

"You're just a bunch of hot air," Anders told her.

Kate ignored him and tried again. But no matter how often she blew, no whistle came.

"See what I mean?" asked Anders. "It's not for girls."

Kate stomped her foot on the floor of the wagon. "Just wait. I'll learn!"

Anders grinned. "Maybe you will at that. You're sure a stubborn little thing."

"Stubborn! Look who's stubborn! You promised Papa you'd help. You're not helping me!"

Anders looked down at Kate, the teasing gone from his eyes. "All right. Maybe you really do need to learn."

Putting both reins in his left hand, he freed up his right. "Watch. Try it this way." Placing his thumb and index finger between his lips, he blew another sharp whistle.

"Show me again," ordered Kate.

Once more Anders put his thumb and index finger between his lips. His whistle sounded strong and clear.

Kate watched closely and tried several times. Still no sound came, only the whoosh of air.

Anders laughed, and Kate felt even more determined. Flipping her long black braid over her shoulder, she blew again. This time a whistle suddenly came.

"I did it!" Kate exclaimed.

For a change Anders looked proud of her. "You must be the first girl in the whole school who whistles that way!"

As they reached the main road, Anders tugged the left rein. Wildfire turned south toward the creamery at Trade Lake.

"Pretty good mare, huh?" Anders asked. As he flicked the reins, Wildfire broke into a trot.

Kate grinned. "Nice looking too."

After a week of staying after school, Kate felt better today. Miss Sundquist had kept her busy sweeping the floor, cleaning shelves, and pounding erasers. It was a relief to be out in the crisp November air.

"Mama hasn't found out," Kate said, as though Anders could read her thoughts.

He did. "You might not be safe yet," he warned. "You still have to get past church tomorrow."

"I'll be all right," answered Kate, her voice confident.

"I mean it," Anders replied. "Someone might talk to Mama."

"Let's not give them the chance. Let's leave the minute church is over."

Anders looked at her strangely. "Kate, what's gotten into you?"

Kate felt the flush of embarrassment. Lifting her chin, she said, "I'm protecting Mama."

"You're protecting your own skin." Anders' voice was grim. "I don't like it. What are you trying to hide? Besides falling through the ice, I mean?"

Instead of meeting his eyes, Kate looked out on the field they were passing. He was hitting too close to what really bothered her.

While working together for a horse and organ, she and Anders had become friends. He had seemed like a real brother. Now for the first time, Kate was hiding something important from him. It made her uneasy, but instead of answering his question she asked, "Have you heard any more about Josie's steer?"

Anders shook his head. "You're trying to get me off track."

But Kate kept on. "What are they going to do?"

Anders shrugged his shoulders. His eyes looked gloomy. "Eleven mouths to feed, and no meat for winter."

"Can her father shoot a deer?"

"Not many around. Used to be a lot of 'em. Settlers lived on the meat they killed. Not anymore."

"How come?" Kate wanted to know.

"They hunted any time of the year, whenever they wished. And Papa says there was heavy logging about twenty-five years ago. Brush grew up really thick afterward."

"So?"

"So deer don't come around anymore. Guess they need more open spaces."

"That's why Josie's worried? Hunting isn't good?"

As Anders nodded, his blond hair fell into his eyes. "Got any ideas?"

Kate shook her head. "Not a one. But Mama won't let them go hungry. She'll send over some of our pig."

Even as she spoke, Kate felt uneasy. What if the thief stole from someone else? What if their own pig disappeared?

"Won't be enough," Anders told her, his voice short. "Josie's got a big family. That animal has to be found soon. Before the thief sells it."

"Or eats it."

Twice they stopped at neighboring farms, picking up more milk cans.

"After I leave these off, I'll go on over," Anders said.

"To Josie's? To see what happened? Or to see Josie?"

Anders grinned. "To see what happened. There's some mighty thick woods near their pasture."

"Could the steer wander away?"

"He could. A lot of 'em do. But there's something bothering Josie. For some reason her father doesn't want to talk about what really happened. I wonder if he's afraid we'd talk too much and tip off the thief."

As they pulled into the Trade Lake Creamery, Anders handed the reins to Kate. "Hold her steady so she doesn't move when I jump down."

Kate grasped the reins. Anders tied the lead rope to a hitching rail, then came back to help Kate down.

"You're going to let me walk the rest of the way?" she asked.

"Yup, won't hurt you a bit." He grinned his lopsided smile. "Usually you walk all four miles." Moving to the back of the wagon, Anders swung down the cans and set them on the creamery platform.

Kate waited until he finished before she said, "You could take me there and still go to Josie's."

Anders shook his head. "Not if I want to get back to help Mama like I promised."

"Sure you can." Before he could object again, Kate climbed back into the wagon.

Anders groaned. "You're a pest! All right, hang on. I'll hurry and make up for it."

As they left the creamery, Anders turned Wildfire south again. They crossed a narrow bridge spanning the Trade River, then reached an open road. Anders flicked the reins, and Wildfire moved out in a trot.

"I'm doing good in my lessons," said Kate.

When she moved to Windy Hill Farm from Minneapolis, Kate thought she was giving up everything, including the organ lessons she wanted. Instead, she now had her own pump organ. To Kate it seemed like a dream come true.

"Still going to be a great organist someday?" asked Anders.

"I'm going to travel around the whole United States, like Jenny Lind."

It seemed a long time since Kate had talked to Papa Nordstrom about the Swedish singer. Now Kate felt afraid to share her dream with Anders. Yet she needed to hope, to speak her dream aloud, and believe it would come true. "I'm going to make people feel good, the way Jenny Lind did when they heard her sing."

"But with an organ instead of a voice," said Anders slyly, and Kate was unaware of the trap he set.

"Yup!" she answered the way Anders would.

"Well then, I guess I'm totin' around the great nightingale of Burnett County."

Suddenly Kate hit his arm, returning his teasing. His hands jerked, and the reins slapped Wildfire's back. Without warning, the mare broke into a gallop.

"Now see what you did!" muttered Anders, pulling hard on the reins.

But Wildfire flattened her ears against her head and tore down the dirt road. "Easy, girl," called Anders. "Easy!"

A large rut loomed ahead of them. Anders pulled on the left rein, and Wildfire swung out. But the right wheel caught in the rut, and the wagon bounced hard.

For a moment Kate thought she'd fall off the seat. The wagon bumped again, then rode it out.

Kate drew a breath of relief, but to her surprise, Anders sounded proud. "Yup! A pretty good horse!"

"Slow down!" she cried as Wildfire again picked up speed. As they flew past trees, the terror within Kate grew. "Stop her!"

# 7

## Trader Carlson's Store

*T*hought you wanted Wildfire to *move*," drawled Anders. Looking away from the road, he grinned down at Kate.

Just then the wagon hit a deep hole.

Kate grabbed hold of the seat and hung on with every ounce of strength. "Stop it!"

Again Anders pulled on the reins. This time Wildfire obeyed. But instead of being frightened, Anders laughed. "Aren't you the one who wanted a ride?"

Before the horse could move again, Kate scrambled down. Once on firm ground, she clutched her music and glared up at Anders. "You better make that horse safe before you take Mama to church tomorrow."

Anders grinned. "She'll be safe all right. I'll just put you where you can't hit my arm."

Kate shook her fist, but Anders laughed. "What a big noise you make for such a little one!"

Drawing herself up, Kate tried to stand as tall as her less than five feet allowed. But her effort was wasted as Anders turned the horse to head back to Josie's farm.

Kate set off at a brisk pace and soon reached the Swedish

settlement called Four Corners. Turning at the crossroads, she came to the church built on the edge of a hill. The road past its doors stretched out like a ribbon, dropping away between trees now bare of leaves.

For a moment Kate stood on the church steps, listening to Mr. Peters play the organ. The chords filled the air, spilling through the closed windows.

Each week Kate looked forward to hearing him play, then playing herself. *Strange,* she thought. *Strange we should move this close to the first hand-pumped organ in the county.*

Sometimes Kate wondered if God planned it all. This past summer she'd often thought about God and even asked for His help. He had seemed real to her. But now He again seemed far away.

Kate knew the change had come this past week. The thought made her uncomfortable, and she pushed it to the back of her mind.

Opening the church door, Kate slipped quietly up the stairs to the balcony. Standing behind Mr. Peters, Kate watched his fingers move across the keyboard, seemingly without effort. His black shoes touched the pedals lightly.

Mr. Peters had come from Sweden to study at Gustavus Adolphus College. When he became choir director and organist at Trade Lake, he married a young woman from the area.

Now came the run Kate hoped for. His left foot lit on the pedals, and his fingers leaped down the scale.

As the music slowed to simple chords, Kate saw Erik. Sitting on the side and near the back of the organ, he pushed a wooden handle up and down. The handle pumped bellows, bringing in air to make the pipes sound.

*How come he's here?* wondered Kate. Always before, there had been another boy. She didn't like to think how Erik might tease after hearing her play.

When Mr. Peters started another piece, Kate moved forward to look at the music.

Mr. Peters heard her and swung around. "Ah, there you are, Kate. A bit early. How are you today?"

As Kate played the first scale, her fingers felt clumsy. With each scale she got worse. Whenever she thought about Erik, she missed notes.

Finally Mr. Peters stopped her. "You can do better than that, Kate. Start over again."

Kate felt the hot flush of embarrassment reach her face. Once more she tried the scale. It sounded even worse.

When she finished, Mr. Peters slid off the bench. Walking around to the side of the organ, he said, "Why don't you take a rest for a few minutes, Erik? I'll pump for a while."

As soon as Erik disappeared, Mr. Peters spoke softly. "Kate, I want you to think of one person who encourages you to play the organ."

Immediately Kate remembered Papa Nordstrom. Soon after she came to Windy Hill Farm, he encouraged her in her dream to be an organist. Where was Papa now? Was he working in a cold, snowy lumber camp? Kate knew he'd like to be home, hearing her play.

Mr. Peters disappeared then, down next to the handle of the organ. But Kate still heard his voice. "Now play."

This time Kate's fingers felt steady upon the keys. She played every note right.

She barely noticed when Erik came back, and Mr. Peters returned to the organ bench. As Kate played the scales and songs she had practiced, she felt a growing excitement.

"You're doing well," said Mr. Peters at last. "Very well for someone who's taken lessons only a few months."

His praise warmed Kate, and he went on. "You have an ear for music. You hear it in your mind, don't you?"

Kate nodded. "When you play, I try to remember the tune. Doesn't everyone do that?"

"No," he said simply. "You're doing what we call playing by ear. When I give you a new piece, you ask how it's supposed to go. I play it for you. You listen and play the way I do. You don't really learn the notes."

Kate was startled, but realized he was right. To her it was the only way to play.

Beneath his moustache, Mr. Peters' lips parted in a smile. "I'm glad you can hear music. But if you depend on listening to someone else play, you'll stop learning. From now on I won't play a new piece for you."

Kate wasn't sure she liked that idea. "That'd be harder."

"It will. But if you learn to read notes, you'll go a lot further."

He stood up, and Kate knew the lesson was over. She felt disappointed and wished he wouldn't make things more difficult. Up to now, playing the organ had been easy, something she wanted to do and just did.

As she headed for the door leading downstairs, Mr. Peters called to her. "You're very gifted, Kate."

Looking back, Kate saw Erik listening. She hoped he wouldn't remember and tease.

Her teacher's next words surprised her. "Because of that gift, I'm going to expect more from you."

*That'll be work!* Kate wanted to tell him. Almost she wished she didn't have a gift for music. Almost, but not quite.

When Kate let herself out of the church, the air was still crisp, yet warmed by the sun directly overhead. She seemed to float on that air instead of a dirt road. Passing the buildings at Four Corners, she headed north.

One moment she felt excited. "Mr. Peters thinks I'm gifted!" She spoke aloud, wanting to make the words real. "Maybe I really will be a great organist!"

The next moment she felt scared, guessing about how much she'd have to learn, how hard it might be.

Lost in thought, she kicked a stone along the road, sending it ahead of her. She tried to whistle, practicing what Anders taught her. Sometimes she could do it. Other times she couldn't.

In the midst of a strong, clear whistle, Kate remembered her mother. Mama would go to church tomorrow. She would talk to people. Someone might tell her what really happened.

The whistle died on Kate's lips. The sunshine seemed to hide beneath the clouds.

Soon Kate crossed the bridge over Trade River and turned toward Trader Carlson's large general store. From miles around, Indians brought their furs, exchanging them for traps and other needed items.

When Kate passed through the door, a bell jangled. As her

eyes adjusted to the dimmer light, she saw a large barrel piled high with apples. Glass jars held hard candy. Bolts of cloth lined one wall. Hardware items filled another.

Passing the candy, Kate wished she dared spend a penny. Instead, she walked on toward the back of the store.

Papa had told her to come here for moccasins. When the weather dropped well below zero, Kate could wear them all day over two pairs of homemade stockings. She'd stay warmer in the often chilly schoolhouse.

Up to now, Mama had always traced Kate's foot on a piece of paper, then taken the paper to a store that sold shoes. As a clerk helped Kate, she felt uncertain, wondering which pair to pick.

Just then, the bell at the door jangled. Kate looked toward the front of the store.

*Stretch!*

For a moment Kate froze, hoping he wouldn't notice her. He hadn't been back to school since the day she fell through the ice. Now Kate wanted to avoid him.

Pretending she didn't see him, she took another pair of moccasins from the clerk. When Kate glanced back up, Stretch stood near a jar of candy. The lid was off.

In that instant, his hand darted out, then back. Looking as though he didn't have a care in the world, he slipped that hand into a pocket.

Kate stared. *Did I see what I think I saw?*

When her clerk left to help someone else, Kate kept watching Stretch. Once more she saw his hand dart forward, then back. This time Kate had no doubt.

But she also remembered Stretch's lazy smile. It had been fun talking with him as they walked down to the lake. To herself Kate started making excuses for Stretch. *He's really not bad, like Anders says.*

Just the same, Kate stayed toward the back of the store, hoping Stretch would leave. The minutes passed slowly. Finally she knew she couldn't wait any longer. Mama expected her home.

Kate picked up the moccasins that fit best, yet gave room for her feet to grow. Walking forward, she paid Trader Carlson. Without looking at Stretch, she hurried from the store.

When Kate reached the road, she walked fast, but her thoughts scurried even faster. Before long, she heard a wagon approaching from behind.

A familiar voice called "Whoa!" to the horses. Then, "Kate!" She looked up into Stretch's lazy smile.

"Want a ride?" he called down.

For a moment Kate stood there, unable to make up her mind. Back in the store she hadn't wanted anything to do with him. Here in the sunlight Stretch seemed harmless, even handsome. And she still had a three-mile walk.

Kate tried to push her uneasiness aside. *Everyone gives rides to everyone else*, she told herself. *That's the country way of doing things*. Besides, she wanted to ask Stretch some questions.

As she climbed into the wagon, Stretch grinned again. Kate remembered why she found him likable. She knew everyone at school felt the same way. Everyone except Anders, Lars, and Erik.

"Where you headed?" Stretch asked.

"Home," Kate answered, hoping for a chance to ask why he left when she needed help. "What're you doing?"

"Goin' home too." Stretch tipped his curly blond head toward the wagon load of long slender tree limbs. "Hauling tamarack for winter. I cut 'em up for firewood. Where's home for you?"

"Windy Hill Farm."

"You part of that family? Your name's O'Connell."

"Yup, and proud of it," said Kate, sounding like Anders. She remembered the day she started Spirit Lake School. Anders had been mean, and she'd gotten even when he introduced her as Katherine Nordstrom. Then it had seemed like a victory to tell Miss Sundquist, "I'm Katherine O'Connell!"

Since then, Kate had grown to love Papa Nordstrom and her new sister and brothers. Every now and then she felt sorry for not using their name. Still, she wanted to remember her Irish daddy.

"O'Connell," repeated Stretch. "That's a strange name."

"Strange, you say? It's Irish. Best name in the world!"

"Irish?" Stretch seemed to muddle it over in his head.

"Yah, sure," said Kate, this time sounding like Papa Nord-strom.

"Well, then," answered Stretch, and somehow the words sounded mean. "You and Harry Blue and Rev. Pickle have some-thing in common."

"What's that?" Kate asked.

"You're the only ones in the whole town of Trade Lake who ain't Scandinavian!"

"So?" asked Kate. "I'm proud of being Irish!"

"Proud, is it?" Stretch gathered both reins in one hand and scratched his head as though thinking hard. "Proud. There oughta be a cure for that."

Kate wasn't sure if he was teasing or being mean. But then as Stretch took the reins in both hands, she saw something.

"How come your hand is blue?"

"Blue?" Stretch looked startled. Looking down, he quickly shifted the reins back and wiped the blue hand on his overalls. But the color didn't wipe off.

"What's it from?" asked Kate.

Stretch's lazy eyes weren't lazy anymore. They'd come alive, like those of a animal trying to run for safety. When he spoke, he seemed to make an effort to sound careless. "Musta worked too hard, sawing down trees." Once more he wiped the hand on his overalls.

*He's lying*, thought Kate. *Lying through his teeth.*

Suddenly Stretch didn't seem very nice. Suddenly Kate wanted to be far away from wherever he was. Seeing a farm-house near at hand, she said, "Just let me off here."

Stretch stopped the horses, and Kate jumped down and away from the wheels. She wanted only one thing: that he would leave.

Yet as Stretch clucked the horses, Kate remembered her ques-tion and called out. "Where'd you go when I fell through the ice?"

Stretch flicked the reins and did not turn.

"Why didn't you help?" Kate hollered after him. But Stretch seemed not to hear.

As the wagon rolled past Kate, it bumped into a hole. For

one moment the tree limbs bounced up. The next moment they dropped back into place. In that one instant Kate saw several wooden boxes set in the wagon.

When the wagon rumbled beyond a rise, Kate slowly followed Stretch down the road. But her thoughts raced far ahead.

*Boxes.* Until that jolt they'd been covered by tree limbs. *What is Stretch trying to hide?*

As Kate walked, she turned it over in her mind. Finally she shrugged her shoulders. *Maybe I'm just imagining things.*

# 8

## *Shadows on the Wall*

When Kate reached home she was still thinking about Stretch. She kept returning to one question: *What's in those boxes?*

She found Lars and Anders hauling water for Saturday night baths. Filling the big washtub the family used for baths took large kettles, heated on top of the wood cookstove.

As Lars built up the fire, he glanced Kate's way, but didn't speak.

"Where's Mama?" Kate asked after a long silence.

"Sleepin'," answered Lars, as untalkative as he'd been all week. "Said you're s'posed to clean the lamps."

On Saturday afternoons it was Kate's job to trim the wicks and wash the glass chimneys of the kerosene lamps. Usually she and Lars spent the time talking. But for five days now Lars had been strangely quiet.

*Ever since I said I wouldn't tell Mama about falling through the ice*, thought Kate, feeling uncomfortable.

A hidden part deep inside Kate knew Lars was right. Yet she didn't want to admit it—even to herself.

"I'm just sparing Mama," she told Lars now.

But Lars didn't answer, and Kate knew that defending herself didn't take away her uneasiness. She sighed just thinking about it. *I don't even like myself anymore.*

Just then Mama came into the kitchen. In spite of her nap, her large blue eyes looked tired. Her knot of golden blond hair, usually centered on top of her head, had slipped sideways.

"Are you all right, Mama?" Kate asked.

Mama smiled. "I just need more sleep because of the baby."

"Mama never sleeps during the day," Kate told Lars when Mama left again. "What'll we do if she gets sick when Papa's gone?"

Lars remained silent, and Kate talked on. "One more reason not to tell her about the ice. I did the right thing."

Still Lars did not speak. Among his freckles his blue eyes looked troubled. The rest of the afternoon and all through supper Kate had to push her uneasiness away.

As she cleaned up the dishes, Anders took out the big round washtub used for baths. Setting the tub on the kitchen floor, he filled it with steaming water.

"Did you see Josie?" Kate asked when she and Anders were alone in the kitchen.

"Yup. She took me out back of their barn. Did you know they tied the steer there?"

Kate shook her head.

"Found out why her father thinks it was stolen. Had a rope around its neck. A good rope that wasn't frayed and worn. It was cut!"

"Poor Josie!" It was one thing to have a steer wander away and become lost. It was something else to have someone steal an animal.

"Did you know they fed that steer almost two years?" Anders sounded angry. "Planned to butcher it about now." He lowered his voice. "We've just got to find that animal before the thief sells it."

Kate had another thought. "What if the thief butchers it? Could Josie's father still recognize it?"

Anders shook his head. "Nope. That's why we have to keep our eyes open."

"But where do we look?"

Anders shrugged his shoulders, but his voice sounded grim. "Don't know. With the disappearing stranger, we found things around here. A steer would probably be hidden in a building."

"People would get mighty upset if we started snooping around their barns and sheds," answered Kate. "It'd look like we don't trust them."

"What's more, people around here are honest. Who would take something like a steer?" Anders was quiet, thinking about it.

Kate began wiping dishes. After a time she broke the silence. "Saw Stretch today."

Anders looked surprised. "You did? Where?"

"First at Trader Carlson's store. Maybe you're right."

"Sure, I'm right," said Anders with his lopsided grin. "Right about what?"

"When you said not to trust him."

"Wel-l-l-l," drawled Anders. "You finally got it figured out. So what gave you that idea?"

When Kate told him about the jar of candy, Anders laughed. "Yup. You caught him with the goods all right. But lots of boys steal candy."

"Including you?"

"Nope. Not anymore. Not since Papa tanned me."

Kate laughed, but then Anders asked another question. "You said first. What's second?"

"Second?"

"Second time you saw him."

Kate wasn't sure she wanted to tell Anders about that. When she described how Stretch came along, offering a ride, Anders interrupted.

"You took a ride with Stretch? After I told you not to go near him?"

"Everyone gives each other rides!"

"So? That doesn't mean you take 'em. 'Specially if you've got pretty blue eyes, long black hair, and you're a girl named Kate!"

"What's wrong with being a girl named Kate?"

"Nothing!" declared Anders. "But there's plenty wrong with a girl named Kate taking a ride from a boy named Stretch! And don't act dumb! You weren't born yesterday!"

"Oh, fiddlesticks!" Kate turned back to the dishes. But a moment later she forgot her own anger at the tall boy with the curly blond hair. "How come you and Erik and Lars are the only ones who don't like Stretch?"

Anders looked at her as though she had lost her mind. "Like I said, 'Dumb girl!' " He stalked out of the kitchen.

In spite of the way Kate talked to Anders, she had some questions of her own. Questions that nagged away at the back of her mind. *What was in those boxes? And why did Stretch have one blue hand?*

As Kate finished the dishes, Tina came in and climbed into the large round tub. Taking the bar of homemade soap, Kate helped the little girl wash her hair.

As youngest, Tina always had her bath first. Then, one by one, each family member took a turn.

"I'm glad I'm second to use the bath water," said Kate. "Lars always gets so dirty."

Usually Tina talked without stopping, using a combination of Swedish and sign language. Tonight she seemed strangely quiet. Soon she finished her bath and pulled on her robe.

Kate started to towel Tina's white blond hair.

The little girl twisted away. "Me do." Pointing to herself, she took the towel from Kate. Her blue eyes didn't quite meet Kate's gaze.

"Something the matter?" Kate asked. Before Mama's marriage to Papa Nordstrom, Kate had always wanted a little sister. Since moving from Minneapolis to Windy Hill Farm, she had grown to love Tina, even though they spoke two different languages. Mama talked to Tina in Swedish, while Kate spoke to her in English.

Once again the five-year-old pointed to herself. "Want no help." Pointing toward Kate, she added, "Liar."

Kate stepped back, feeling as though she'd been struck on the cheek. "A liar?"

Tina nodded, her blue eyes solemn. "Lars said—" Stopping midsentence, Tina clapped her hand over her mouth.

"Oh ho!" Kate said, as though ready to pounce. "So tattletale Lars has been talking?"

Tina's eyes looked scared. She backed away from Kate and ran from the room.

As the door between the kitchen and dining room slammed in her face, Kate stopped. The little girl would go to Mama. She wouldn't say what was wrong. But she'd sit close to Mama so Kate couldn't talk.

*Dumb sister!* thought Kate for the first time since Mama married Mr. Nordstrom.

Trying to push aside her angry feelings, Kate added hot water to the tub, undressed, and climbed in. Crossing her legs at the ankles, she slid under the water as far as possible.

Though short for her age, she found it harder all the time to fit into the tub. Yet Kate looked forward to her once-a-week bath. Usually the warm soapy water felt good.

Tonight thoughts of Lars kept coming back. "Tattletale!" Kate muttered aloud. "What if he tells Mama?"

All week Lars had stayed away from Kate. Whenever they walked to and from school, he ran ahead, or poked along behind. It hurt Kate.

On her first cold and muddy ride to Windy Hill Farm, Lars had helped her. And when Anders didn't speak to her during their first walk to school, Lars did.

As Kate washed her long black hair, she thought about it. *Lars has been more than a friend. He's been a brother. That is, until now.*

A knock on the door interrupted her thoughts. "Are you almost done, Kate?" called Mama.

Quickly Kate stepped out of the water. "In a minute!" she answered, pulling on her robe.

As Kate entered the dining room, Mama added wood to the fire. She straightened, and Kate saw that Mama was losing her slim waist.

"Tina says we haven't sung together since Papa left," Mama told Kate. "Will you play for us?"

Kate looked at Tina, and the little girl looked down. *It's not the singing she wants*, Kate thought. *She doesn't want to go to bed.*

In the front room Kate sat down at her prized organ and picked out the simple songs she knew how to play. Soon she discovered she was right. Tina sang halfheartedly.

As Lars finished his bath and entered the room in a clean shirt and overalls, Kate saw him look at Tina. The little girl grinned, and Kate wondered, *What's up?*

They were still singing when Anders came in, also in clean clothes, and with his thatch of straight blond hair still wet. By now Kate had played every song she knew and started over again. Feeling uneasy, she stopped, and twirled around on the organ stool.

This time she caught Lars in a long slow wink in Anders' direction.

Kate's thoughts were grim. *They're planning something. All this talk about responsibility. Fiddlesticks!*

For the first time in many months she felt shut out by the other children. Since she and Anders had solved the mystery of the disappearing stranger, Kate had been part of every plan. Now she felt empty with loneliness.

"Time for bed, Tina," Mama said.

Tina stood up, walked over to Kate, and tugged her hand. In that moment Kate felt better. Tina seemed her old self.

Lighting a candle, Kate picked up the holder and led Tina to the hallway. Wavering shadows danced on the walls as they climbed the stairs. As Kate and Tina entered the bedroom they shared, more shadows reached out from the corners. The darkness of the November night seemed to touch them. So did the cold.

Kate shivered and pointed to the bed. "Hop in and I'll sing one more song." It had become their ritual, one that helped the little girl go to sleep.

But in spite of the cold Tina looked around at the shadows and refused to climb into bed. Hugging herself, she hopped up and down on bare feet.

"Get in," said Kate impatiently. "You won't warm up until you do."

"Cold," said Tina, one of the few English words she knew. "Cold!" The word ended in a wail.

"You're right," said Kate, feeling the chill around her. Only a little heat from the wood stove had come through the grate in the floor. "Just a minute. I'll be right back."

Setting the candle holder on a small table, Kate hurried down to the kitchen. There she took one of the flatirons heating on the cookstove. Wrapping it in a cloth, Kate returned to Tina. "Now your feet will be warm."

In the dim light Kate lifted the quilt. As she slid the iron between the flannel sheets used in winter, Kate touched something.

When she jumped, Tina snickered. Yet Kate saw only innocence on the little girl's face.

Unwilling to take a chance, Kate turned the quilt back from the top. Then she saw what she had felt—a small wooden box.

A ribbon tied around the box held a silk flower to the top. Kate recognized the flower from one of Mama's old hats.

"Surprise for you, Tina." Kate held out the box to the little girl.

But Tina put her hands behind her back. "Pretty," she said. "You." She pointed to Kate.

By now Kate was curious. Setting the box on the table, she untied the ribbon, lifted the flower, and opened the lid.

A white sheet of paper filled the top of the box. Moving the candle close, Kate read the carefully printed words.

# Pretty on the outside.

# Like this on the inside.

In the semidarkness Kate squinted, wondering if she'd read correctly. She peered at the words.

Curious, Kate picked up the paper. Seeing what was underneath, she shrieked. "Oh, oh, oh!" She edged back from the box.

Tina giggled, but in her terror Kate barely heard. Again she screamed.

Footsteps pounded up the stairs. Anders, then Lars and Mama, tore into the room.

"What on earth is wrong?" asked Mama.

Kate was trembling now. "Oh, it's awful—so awful!"

# 9

## *Escape!*

$A$nders and Lars stood at the door, and Mama started toward the box. Anders moved quickly.

"Just a minute, Mama." He closed the box before she could look inside.

"But what is it?" she asked.

"A dead mouse!" shrieked Kate, starting to cry. Collapsing on a chair, she put her hands over her face and wept into them.

"A dead mouse?" Mama drew herself up to her full height. "Why is there a dead mouse in this box?"

"Oh, I never should have done it!" sobbed Kate.

"Never should have done *what*, young lady?"

Kate bit her lip, but it was too late. Mama demanded an answer.

"I was going to be responsible, so you wouldn't worry." Kate's words ended on a wail, broken by another sob. "I'm sorry, Mama."

"Sorry for *what*? I don't know what you've done."

Kate still trembled from her look at the mouse. "There isn't anything in the whole world, not *anything* I hate more than mice!"

"I understand that," Mama said dryly. "Now tell me what this is all about."

Kate drew a deep breath. "I fell through the ice on Spirit Lake." She shivered, just remembering the cold water. Then her fear came back. Fear of the dark water, of that moment when she couldn't find the hole in the ice. Yet even more, Kate felt afraid of what Mama would think.

"You fell through the ice, and didn't *tell* me?" Mama spoke in a jumble of Swedish and English.

Kate stumbled her way through the story.

"But why didn't you tell me before?" Mama asked again.

"I was afraid of what you'd say," Kate answered, her voice small.

"I'd say, 'Thank God! You're all right!' " Mama exclaimed.

But Kate knew she had to go on. Her voice sounded even smaller. "So I told you I was helping Miss Sundquist after school."

"You told me a lie, you mean," said Mama sternly.

Biting her lip to keep from crying again, Kate nodded. "I told you a lie, Mama. I'm sorry."

"You're sorry!" Mama snapped. "You're sorry?" Her voice grew in volume with every word. "You lie to your mama, and you're sorry? That's even worse than disobeying your teacher! Worse than going down to the lake!"

Numbly Kate nodded, her eyes downcast, her toe tracing a pattern on the wood floor.

"Yes, Mama. I know, Mama. I'm sorry, Mama."

Mama sighed, and when she spoke again, her voice was quiet with sadness. "Kate, look at me."

Kate looked up. In the candlelight she saw Mama's eyes glisten with tears.

"I never thought my daughter would lie to me," said Mama softly, each word filled with pain.

Kate looked down, no longer able to meet Mama's eyes.

But Mama went on. "Kate, I forgive you. But you must ask God to forgive you. You will also spend two hours in your room every afternoon for a week. You'll go there as soon as you come home from school."

"Oh, Mama!" cried Kate. "I've already been punished!"

"You've been punished for disobedience." Mama's voice was firm. "This is for lying."

Without another word she turned and walked slowly from the room. Her footsteps sounded heavy on the stairs.

Kate looked at Lars. When his gaze slid sideways, she knew he was the guilty one. "You planned this!" Kate accused.

"He was worried about your character," remarked Anders, a gleam of laughter in his eyes.

"You're just as mean as he is!" stormed Kate. She turned on Tina. "You were in on this too!"

Kate glared at all of them. "I can't bear the sight of you!"

"Aw, com'on, Kate," Anders said. "You know you were wrong."

Without answering, Kate ran from the room and headed down the stairs. Snatching up her coat, she pulled it on over her robe and hurried outside. She wanted to be alone, and she knew the best place. A tucked-away spot in the haymow.

————

On Monday Kate's week of punishment started. "You must stay in your room for two hours each day," Mama told her. "You can't read or do your schoolwork."

"Not even lessons?"

Mama's face was grim. "You must think about the seriousness of lying."

And that's what Kate did—for the first fifteen minutes. *I really am sorry*, she thought, promising herself she'd never lie again.

Halfheartedly she began knitting mittens to replace the ones she'd lost in the lake. But at the end of an hour and a half she could no longer sit still. Restlessly, Kate moved around from one window to the next.

The room she and Tina shared was on the front end of the house with windows facing two directions. On one side, windows overlooked the porch roof and the wagon track that circled the front and side of the house. Beyond that track lay a plowed field with tall oaks at its edge.

On another side, the room had two more windows. From

one of these, Kate saw the wagon track that forked to the right, dropping down the hill to the shores of Rice Lake. That track led through the woods to Spirit Lake School.

A large pine stood close to the second window on that side. Like spokes of a wheel, the branches grew around the trunk and swayed gently in the wind. The needles looked soft and inviting.

Pushing up the window, Kate inspected the tree. Papa had told her it was called a *white pine*, even though its needles were green. Some of the branches grew past the window, almost touching the house. The nearest branch looked sturdy and easy to reach. The next ones seemed like stair steps, descending down the tree.

Kate bit her lip, thinking about it. For a long time she stood there, looking at the branches, then at the ground.

The base of the huge trunk stood near the kitchen door and Mama's watchful eye. "But I could go down the other side of the tree," Kate told herself as an idea took shape. "No one would see."

She was still arguing with herself when Tina rapped, then poked her white-blond head around the half-open door. "Mama says time up." By now Kate knew enough Swedish to understand.

The second morning of Kate's week of imprisonment dawned unusually warm for November. All day the temperature climbed. At school the children talked about the warm spell, eager for afternoon classes to end.

"Ice is going to melt on the lakes," Anders told Kate on their way home from school.

As she started her two hours of punishment, Kate discovered Anders was right. From her bedroom window, she gazed across Rice Lake. Open water surrounded the ice.

Kate longed for only one thing—to be outside on this beautiful day. For a time she stood at the window closest to the white pine, looking up and down the trunk. Again she checked the size of the branches and the spacing between them.

In Minneapolis she'd been a good tree climber. Now Kate felt eager to be out in the sun.

"I can do it," she told herself, quietly lifting the window closest to the tree. Leaning out, she judged the distance carefully. "I'm sure I can do it."

But Kate knew that she shouldn't. Pulling back inside, she closed the window and sat down on the bed. She stayed there only a minute.

Slowly, quietly, she lifted the window. She reached out for the nearest branch and found it an easy distance away.

Grabbing hold of the limb, Kate climbed onto the windowsill. Stretching down her foot, she felt the next lowest branch. As she stepped onto it, the limb bent under her weight. Carefully Kate worked her way over to the trunk.

Once there, she crawled around to the side away from the house. Branch by branch, Kate let herself down the tree.

Dropping to the ground, she stood behind the large trunk, catching her breath. Seeing no one, she slipped across the grass to the wagon track leading into the woods. Soon the hill dropped sharply away. Kate knew it hid her from view.

Yet even here she was not safe. Anders or Lars could come along. Kate hurried down the trail, wanting only to put distance between herself and the house.

Partway to school, she came to the large oak and the clump of birch that she remembered. Off to her right the trees thinned out. As Kate left the trail, she made her way around heavy underbrush. There she found the big rock she sought.

As she climbed onto it, Kate remembered her first day at Spirit Lake School. She'd seen the disappearing stranger from here. In the time since, she hadn't told anyone about the rock.

"It's my special secret," Kate said to herself now. She felt the rock belonged to her.

Nearby, on the side away from the path, the hill sloped sharply away. Long brown marsh grass and small trees filled the area between her and Rice Lake. Now the trees were bare of leaves, and Kate looked beyond them to the west. The sun shone on the ice and open water.

For a time Kate stood there, glad to be outside. A warm breeze stirred the hair that had slipped out of her braid into her face. But gradually the wind grew cold. Kate turned away, looking for shelter.

Small tree limbs lay on the ground from an oak Papa and Anders had sawed up that fall. Seeing the branches, Kate had an idea.

Then she noticed the sun. In the November afternoon it hovered dangerously close to the horizon. Time to be home!

Walking quickly, Kate headed back to Windy Hill Farm. By the time she entered the yard, she was panting. Moving quietly across the grass, she reached the tree, climbed up, and slipped through the window. Closing it, she sat down to catch her breath.

Moments later, Tina knocked, then pushed open the door.

Kate's time of punishment for that day was over. But Tina had a question, one she asked in her own sign language. As she pointed to Kate, the little girl asked, "Do?" which meant, "What have you been doing up here?"

Kate felt herself flush. She didn't want to lie to her little sister.

But Tina didn't wait for an answer. "Supper," she said. Tugging Kate's hand, she urged her to hurry.

---

When Kate returned home from school the next afternoon, the weather was still unusually warm. For a few minutes Kate debated about what to do. It wasn't long before she slipped out of her room and down the tree. Once again she headed for the big rock. On the way there she heard a cowbell.

Following the sound, Kate discovered a cow wandering through the woods, nibbling whatever grass she found. Kate recognized her.

"Bessie!" she exclaimed, and the cow raised her head. She belonged to Josie's family.

"What're you doing here?" Kate asked, as if the cow could answer.

Lunging at her, Kate tried to catch the rope around Bessie's neck. Bessie edged away. Kate tried again and succeeded.

As she hung on to the rope, Kate wondered what to do next. "If I leave you here, you'll get lost again," she told the cow. "Hard telling when Josie's family will find you."

But Josie lived on the far side of the woods, beyond Spirit

Lake School. "If I take you home, can I get back in time?"

The cow's brown eyes rolled as she mooed her response.

Kate thought of the steer the family had already lost. Sighing, she tugged at the rope. "You don't give me much choice, old Bess."

As Kate started down the trail, the cow turned in the opposite direction. Kate tugged again, but the cow was stubborn and swung her head back and forth. Her large body seemed to loom above Kate.

For a moment Kate felt afraid. Though people in Minneapolis sometimes kept cows in their backyard, she had seldom been close to them. At the same time, she didn't want the Swenson family to have more trouble.

Stepping as far away from the hooves as she could, Kate pulled on the rope with all her strength. "Come on, Bessie!"

This time the cow moved step-by-slow-step in the direction Kate wanted. But the cow had one pace—her own. Precious minutes ticked away as Bessie poked along, reaching for any grass along the trail.

To Kate it seemed forever before she reached Josie's barnyard. There she found her friend's father.

*"Tack! Tack!"* he said. The word sounded like the tock of a clock, but Kate knew it was the Swedish "thank you."

Quickly she slipped away. Once out of Mr. Swenson's sight, Kate started running. Already the woods were dim. When she came to Rice Lake and the opening in the trees, Kate saw the last bit of orange sun dip below the horizon.

Reaching the large pine, she tried to catch her breath. Still panting, she scrambled up the tree and slipped through the window.

As Kate's feet touched the bedroom floor, a voice spoke from the shadows. A voice that said, "Kate!"

# 10

## *Down in the Cellar*

*K*ate spun around.

Tina spoke again from the shadows. "What are you doing?" she asked in Swedish. But Kate recognized the words. She'd often heard them from Anders.

"What are *you* doing, you mean? Spying on me?" Kate replied in English.

As her eyes adjusted to the dim light, Kate saw Tina's hurt look. Though she probably didn't understand the words, Tina seemed to catch the sound. Never before had Kate been so mean to the little girl—not even when discovering the mouse.

Tina's lower lip quivered. She pointed to herself, then to the window and the branch outside. She seemed to ask, "Take me with next time."

In the sign language they'd learned to use, Tina moved her hands and feet as though climbing down the tree. She seemed to believe "I'm big enough."

Angrily, Kate shook her head.

Tina answered in Swedish. "Mama's going to be mad."

Kate recognized those words too. Placing her fingers across Tina's lips, Kate pointed to the door, and shook her head. Then she held up her fist and shook it. "You're not going to tell, are you?"

Tina understood the message. Her lip quivered again, and her eyes filled with tears. Turning her back on Kate, she stalked from the room.

Instantly Kate felt awful. But it was too late. She couldn't bring back the words.

———

When Kate got home from school the next day, it was again warm and sunny. She was holding the upper branch, ready to step down on the lower one, when she heard a loud knock on the door.

"Kate!" called a voice. It was Tina.

Quickly Kate stepped back inside. She lowered the window as Tina shouted again.

"I'm coming, I'm coming!" Kate called back. "What do you want?" she asked, opening the door.

Tina's white-blond hair wisped around her face and her blue eyes danced. She pointed to Kate, then outside, as if to say, "You get out!"

Down in the kitchen, Mama had a basket of food ready. "Anders tells me that Mrs. Berglund has been sick," she told Kate when she came. "He's hitching up Wildfire. I want you to go along and help in any way needed."

"Who's Mrs. Berglund?" asked Kate, always surprised at the number of people her mother knew.

"She's a widow living alone," explained Mama. "Her son works in St. Paul."

"If I go, does it count for one of my days of punishment?" asked Kate.

"Sorry, but things don't work that way," Mama told her, and Kate wished she hadn't asked.

"We'll see how much you manage to help Mrs. Berglund," Mama went on.

Afraid Mama would change her mind and not let her go, Kate pulled on her coat and hurried out the door.

On the way to the farm, she and Anders talked again about Stretch.

"There's something that bothers me," Kate began. "Last Saturday when I saw him, one of his hands was blue."

"Blue?" Anders was curious. "You're sure? Maybe you were just seeing things."

Remembering how Anders felt about her taking a ride, Kate didn't want to admit she'd seen Stretch's hand close up. "I'm sure," she answered. "And only his right hand. He said he'd been working hard, cutting trees. But that wouldn't make a hand blue, would it?"

"Nope," said Anders. His eyes looked puzzled. "But what would?"

The wagon ride went too fast to Kate's way of thinking.

As they drove into the farmyard, Anders told Kate about Mrs. Berglund. "She's old. Really old. Her son doesn't want her to live here alone. She says, 'It's my home. I'll stay as long as I can!' So she keeps a cow and chickens and a garden."

Mrs. Berglund met them at the door. With white hair and twinkling eyes, she smiled like a young person. The lines around her eyes crinkled as though she laughed often. She made Kate feel completely at home.

"*Tack, tack,*" she said in the Swedish "thank you" as Kate brought in the basket of food. "But you must have some with me."

Soon Mrs. Berglund found the cookies. "Just as I thought. I'm sure these are for you and Anders."

"But Mama says I'm supposed to help you," answered Kate.

"You are," said Mrs. Berglund firmly. "I'm much better today. I'm ready to sit down and talk."

Shuffling across the kitchen, she took three glasses from the cupboard.

"I'll get the milk," offered Kate quickly. Pulling on her coat, she headed toward the door, expecting the milk to be in the well as it was at home.

But Mrs. Berglund stopped her. "This time of year I put it in the cellar."

Going to one side of the kitchen, Mrs. Berglund pointed to a ring in the floor. Kate tugged at the ring, surprised at how easily the trapdoor lifted.

Pulling it back, Kate saw stairs that led down into darkness.

For a moment she hesitated, wondering if there were mice.

"It's on the ledge to your right," directed Mrs. Berglund.

Kate knew she'd have to go down whether she liked it or not. Slowly she stepped onto the stairway.

Mrs. Berglund stopped her. "You better take a candle."

As she waited for the old woman to light one, Kate stared into the semidarkness. Nearby, on both sides of the stairs, she saw earth walls.

Mrs. Berglund handed her the candle, and Kate held it out in front of her. Carefully, she continued down the steps. The wood boards creaked beneath her feet. Something that sounded like a mouse scurried away. Kate's heart pounded into her throat.

She listened until the noise quit, then knew she had to go on. As she reached the dirt floor at the bottom of the steps, Kate felt cooler air. Holding the candle high, she looked around.

The dim light didn't reach far enough into the small room, but she guessed it was built only under the kitchen. Peering into the darkness, Kate saw that one side had a boarded-off section and large bins. The other walls seemed to have a wide ledge about three feet from the ground.

A covered pail stood on the ledge closest to the stairs. It looked as though it held milk, and she picked it up.

Starting toward the steps, Kate felt a sudden breath of cold air. Wondering about it, she turned in the direction from which it came. Without warning, her candle flickered, then blew out.

She gasped. As the blackness closed around her, Kate's terror of mice returned.

For a moment she stood there, wanting to drop the milk and the worthless candle. She wanted only the warm, safe kitchen.

Then she heard Mrs. Berglund's voice. "Kate? Did you find the milk?"

Turning to the voice, Kate saw the patch of daylight at the top of the steps. Taking care not to spill the milk, she took a small step forward. As she felt her way, her ankle bumped into the bottom stair.

Stepping onto it, Kate hurried up into the kitchen. The heat of the cookstove reached out. Sunlight streamed through the windows.

As Kate set the milk on the kitchen table, Anders came in. He looked at her strangely.

Quickly Kate pushed back the strands of hair that fell into her face. Her voice slightly unsteady, she asked Mrs. Berglund, "Should I pour the milk?"

Again Kate caught Anders looking at her.

The old woman seemed to see the same thing. "Kate, how did you get so dirty going down for milk?" she asked.

Anders grinned. "That's just the way she is, Mrs. Berglund." His voice sounded dead serious.

Reaching up, Kate rubbed her cheek. Sure enough, her hand came away gritty.

Going to the basin near the kitchen door, Kate washed her face and hands, then threw the dirty water outside. But her questions didn't disappear with the wash water.

"Mrs. Berglund used to be a church organist," Anders told Kate when she returned to the table.

"You did?" Kate was glad to find someone else who played the organ. "Why did you stop?"

Mrs. Berglund's smile disappeared. She held out her hands.

Though they were small, the joints on her fingers were large. Some of the fingers turned in the wrong direction, and both hands bent sideways.

Kate felt embarrassed that she'd asked. "I'm sorry. What is it?"

"Arthritis," Mrs. Berglund said simply. "Don't be embarrassed. Over the years my hands just turned this way."

"But don't you feel bad?" Kate's words tumbled out before she could stop them. "Don't you want to keep playing?"

"Oh yes," answered Mrs. Berglund. "With all my heart I want to play. I want to play for the Lord."

"For the Lord?" Kate asked. She'd never heard of anyone doing that.

"Yah," said Mrs. Berglund, sounding as Swedish as her name. "I like to play hymns that help people think about God."

She smiled, and beneath her blue eyes, her cheeks crinkled. "I used to have a dream. I used to wish for a daughter."

"A daughter?" Kate wanted to know more.

"Or someone I could teach to play the same way."

She fell silent then, and Kate was still. She wished she could say, "I want to play for the Lord." Yet Kate knew it wasn't true, and she could not speak.

Even Anders was quiet.

On the way home Anders once again drove faster than Kate liked.

"Stop it!" Kate exclaimed.

"What's the matter? Are you a scaredy-cat?"

"Of course not!" Kate protested, afraid of what he'd think if she admitted her fear. She hesitated, searching for a reason, and finally said, "It's not good for Wildfire."

Anders hooted. "Wildfire loves it. Just watch."

He slapped the reins. Kate's head jerked back as the mare broke into a gallop.

Filled with panic, she braced her feet and hung on to the wagon seat.

Anders laughed. "You *are* a scaredy-cat!"

"No, I'm not!" she stormed. Yet she clutched the seat until her fingers ached.

Then she saw the turn ahead. "Slow down!" she cried out.

Instead, Anders urged the mare on. Wildfire held true to her name. She ran as swift as a fire licking across dry grass in a high wind.

Kate held her breath, too afraid even to cry out.

# 11

## Bad News

*J*ust before they reached the turn, Anders reined back. As they rounded the corner safely, Kate felt shaken. "I'm telling Mama!"

"So now we have a tattletale," accused Anders. "Who are you to talk?"

"We're not supposed to worry Mama!" Kate cried out.

"And you've already worried her enough!"

For that Kate had no answer, knowing he spoke the truth. Yet she didn't stay quiet long. "Will you teach me how to handle Wildfire?"

"Nope," answered Anders flatly.

"With Papa gone, someone else should know."

Anders sighed. "Kate, you are a pest! I said *no*."

But her mind was made up. All the way home she teased him until he gave in.

When they pulled up outside the Windy Hill barn, Anders climbed down. In the growing dusk he lit a farm lantern. "All right, you win."

His voice sounded as unwilling as his face looked. "Help me unharness her. Watch how it's supposed to be done."

Going first to one side, then the other, Anders unhooked the straps holding Wildfire to the wagon shafts. Together they led the mare into her stall.

There Anders taught Kate to unbuckle the belly strap and pull off the harness. "Don't tangle it. Keep it looped over your arm." Then, "Hang it up." Anders tipped his head toward hooks along the wall.

There Kate met her first problem. She couldn't reach the hooks. Stretching as tall as possible, she threw the harness up until it caught.

Next Anders showed her how to take off the bridle. "Easy on her mouth. Don't hurt her, and she'll like you more."

As he put his hand along Wildfire's big teeth, Kate wondered if she could ever get that close to the mare's mouth. Wildfire let the bit drop out, and Anders took the bridle. Handing Kate the halter, he said, "Slip it over her head."

Kate reached high, but couldn't make it.

"What a shorty!" Anders teased. Just the same, he showed Kate what to do. "See that board in the stall?"

Kate squinted in the dim light. Sure enough, in the wall next to the feed trough, one board stuck out just a bit. Using it as a step, Kate grabbed the edge of the trough and pulled herself up.

Wrapping her arm around a corner pole, she reached forward and slipped the halter over Wildfire's head.

"Give her some oats," Anders ordered next. "Let her get to know you."

By the time they left the barn, Kate felt good about what she'd learned. She felt even better when Anders said, "You're strong, Kate. For a girl, that is. Maybe you'll handle it after all."

From Anders that was rare praise.

————

The next morning something happened that made them forget even Josie's steer for a time.

As usual, Erik and his sister joined Anders, Kate, and Lars on the way to school. Erik had bad news. "Someone robbed us!" he told them.

Kate stopped in the middle of the trail. "What did they take?"

"All our raspberries, our strawberries, and every single jar of blueberries!" Erik exclaimed, his voice angry.

Something in Kate couldn't believe the bad news. "Your fruit for the whole winter?"

Erik's nod was grim. "We picked and picked!" He kicked a branch from the path as though taking his anger out on the thief.

During the summer Kate and Anders and Lars had also picked wild berries in the woods around their farm. Kate knew the terrible mosquitoes and the bites that itched long afterward. She could still feel the long sharp branches that had torn her clothing and left painful scratches on her arms and legs.

"We even drove the wagon out to the sand barrens," Erik went on. "All of us picked a whole day! We filled every bucket we had with blueberries."

"And canned all of them?"

Erik's sister Chrissy answered. "Everything we didn't eat right away. Every jar is gone!" Her eyes filled with misery. "Mama cried."

"The day you moved, I saw you put jars in the root cellar," said Kate.

Unlike the cellar under Mrs. Berglund's house, Erik's root cellar was similar to the one on the Nordstrom farm. A small dark room built into the side of a hill, it had dirt walls and roof. On both cold and warm days that dirt protected the food.

"Any idea when it happened?" asked Anders.

Erik shrugged. "Don't know. When we moved in, we put some jars in the house. Enough for this week. We put everything else in the root cellar. It doesn't freeze there if we're gone and the fire goes out."

"So no one's been to the cellar for a week?"

Erik shook his head. "Not since we moved in."

Then Kate had another thought. Like other farm families, the Nordstroms brought all they grew in their garden into the root cellar. "What about your potatoes and carrots and squash?"

"They're gone too," said Erik gloomily. "All that hard work weeding and watering! Picking the food and bringing it in. And where can we even look to find it?"

Anders and Kate stared at Erik, knowing the food could be almost any place, even dumped off in the woods.

"There's another thing," said Erik, his voice grim. "What if the thief doesn't take care of the food? If the vegetables froze, they'd be wrecked. Then what good would it do to find 'em?"

Deep inside, Kate hurt for Erik and his family. This time of year every night dropped below freezing. And when it grew really cold, only an hour, even in daytime, could spoil all the food.

"Were there any clues at all?" she asked.

"Just one thing, and we almost missed that. Close to the road there was one broken canning jar. I almost stepped on the glass. Looked like it had blueberries in it."

Kate had never seen Erik so discouraged. But they all knew the worst was ahead. Erik's father couldn't go out to buy fruit and vegetables. Farm families lived on what they grew, then stored.

"What'll we eat this winter?" Erik asked, his voice worried.

Deep inside Kate, a knot formed. As though it was yesterday she recalled the year after Daddy O'Connell died. She remembered what it was like not having enough money for food. What could be more awful than trying to live a whole winter without fruit or vegetables?

"We'll give you some of ours," she answered, knowing Mama wouldn't let anyone go hungry if she could help it.

Erik looked grateful, but a moment later asked, "What if the thief comes to your root cellar? What if he takes *your* food?"

Kate saw the quick look that crossed Anders' face.

"For all we know, he's been there already!" he exclaimed.

"I hope not," said Erik grimly. "I sure hope not."

Anders stopped in the middle of the path. "I'm going home, Kate. Tell Teacher I had to work."

Without another word, Anders broke into a run, heading back toward Windy Hill Farm.

# 12

## Up the Pine Tree

At recess time Anders showed up at school. "So far we're all right," he told Kate and Erik. They were out on the playground where other children couldn't hear. "I found an old padlock and locked the root cellar."

"But what about our pig?" asked Kate, feeling uneasy. Before Papa left, he had butchered and put it in the summer kitchen. There it stayed frozen, and Anders would saw off a piece from time to time for them to eat.

Anders looked just as worried as Kate felt. "Couldn't find another lock. If we take the pig into the house, the meat will thaw out and spoil."

When school ended that afternoon, the unusually warm weather still held. "Last two hours of punishment!" Kate told herself, glad her week was almost over.

After her freedom of the day before, Kate found the idea of staying indoors especially terrible. This time she didn't argue with herself even one second. She closed her bedroom door, went to the window, and pulled it up.

Taking hold of the nearest branch, Kate stepped out, then climbed from limb to limb. Partway down the pine tree, she heard a sound and looked up.

Tina!

Tina, reaching for the closest branch!

Tina, ready to climb out the window!

Terror shot through Kate. Before she could move, Tina clutched the limb and swung out.

But her shorter legs did not reach the branch below as Kate's had done. Tina hung in midair, her feet dangling.

Kate froze, unable to speak or move. Then she knew she must. Somehow she called out. "Hang on, Tina!"

Scrambling back up the tree, she saw the terror in Tina's eyes.

"Hang on!" Kate shouted again. The little girl's feet swung in the air.

As she climbed onto the limb beneath Tina, Kate caught a glimpse of the ground far below. *That's where she'd land*. Kate felt dizzy thinking about it.

Trying not to look at the ground, Kate waited for her head to clear. Then she curled her arm around the branch to which Tina clung. Her feet on the limb below, Kate stood up.

As she edged out on the branch, it bent down beneath her weight. *What if it breaks?*

At the same time Tina started to tremble. Her legs swung wide.

Panic washed over Kate like a wave. *How long can she hang on?*

Just as Kate reached her, Tina shrieked. As she dropped, Kate's free arm went around her.

Kate gasped under Tina's weight. "Don't move," she warned, knowing she couldn't hold the five-year-old long.

Then Kate remembered that Tina didn't understand much English.

For a moment Kate stood there, hanging on with all her strength. She wondered if she'd fall just from the terror of it. Tina would go with her.

Then Kate thought of Erik, and how he talked her out of the icy lake.

"Put your hands up, Tina," said Kate, wanting to motion with her head. She felt afraid to move even that much.

But Tina did not raise her hands.

"Grab the branch again." Kate spoke slowly, trying to keep her voice steady.

Tina trembled, but seemed to understand. While Kate held her, the little girl reached up and clutched the branch.

As some of Tina's weight shifted off Kate's arm, she felt the relief. "Trunk," she said, still hoping Tina understood.

One arm around the little girl, the other clinging to the upper branch, Kate slowly took a step.

Again Tina trembled. Yet she moved her hands, one by one. Kate slid her feet along the lower branch.

It seemed to take forever, but at last they reached the trunk.

As Kate caught her breath, her panic returned. *I don't have a free hand. I can't grab a new branch without letting go of the old one.*

She stood there, wondering how to go on, her fear making it hard to think. But then Kate knew what to do. Leaning toward the little girl, she pushed Tina against the trunk. Slowly she let Tina's body drop. At last the five-year-old sat on the branch on which Kate stood.

Crouching behind Tina, Kate reached out, searching for a limb close enough for the smaller girl.

Tina watched. Each time Kate changed position, Tina put her hands and feet in the place Kate left. At last they reached the lowest branch and dropped to the ground.

"Oh, Tina!" Kate exclaimed, giving her such a tight hug that the younger girl squealed.

As they rested on the grass, Kate began to shake. One picture stayed in her mind. Tina dangling from the tree, ready to fall to the ground below.

Kate reached out to feel that ground, glad that she and Tina sat upon it. In that moment Kate felt glad even for the dead, brown grass of autumn. But her trembling would not stop. She felt overwhelmed with what could have happened.

At last Kate stood up. Afraid she'd change her mind, she headed for the house. As she stalked through the kitchen door, Tina followed.

Mama looked as though she'd just wakened from a nap. "Kate! What are you doing out of your room?"

Before Mama could utter another word, Kate spoke. "Mama, I ask your forgiveness." In her determination to confess, Kate's voice sounded bold.

Mama looked startled. "For lying, Kate?"

"No—I mean, yes." Kate stumbled over the words. She had almost forgotten why she was being punished. "For that too."

She flipped her braid over her shoulder and lifted her head. "I ask forgiveness for climbing down the tree when I was supposed to stay in my room."

Mama opened her mouth to speak. Then, seeming to think better of it, she closed her lips and waited.

Kate swallowed around the lump in her throat. "I ask forgiveness for doing something Tina tried to follow."

Mama turned white. "Tina did *what*?"

"She climbed out the window into the tree."

"And she climbed down the tree by herself?"

"No, Mama. She hung from the tree. She couldn't reach the next branch."

Mama moved to a chair and quickly sat down.

"I'm sorry, Mama," said Kate again. Her lower lip trembled. Tears welled up in her eyes and spilled onto her cheeks. Sobs tore at her body, coming from deep within.

Mama reached out for her. "Oh, Kate!"

There was barely enough room on Mama's lap. For a moment Kate thought, *I'm too old to sit here.*

But Mama smelled like newly baked rolls and apple pie. Her arms felt warm and good. Within their safety, Kate broke down completely. "Oh, Mama, I'm so awful!"

"Yah," Mama said quietly, seeming to agree. Hearing Mama, Kate cried even harder.

Yet Mama stroked Kate's cheek, as though she was thinking. When she spoke, her voice sounded stronger. "Yah, we are all awful, Kate."

Through her sobbing, Kate heard the words. But it took a moment before she really heard them. Then she sniffled and pulled back, looking up.

"*You* are awful, Mama?" Kate couldn't believe she'd heard right.

"Yah, I am awful, Kate." Mama handed her a handkerchief.

"But I don't understand. You always seem perfect."

Mama shook her head. "In the whole world no one is perfect."

"No one?"

"No one." Mama was certain about that. "But you remember, Kate. God did something for all of us."

As she held Kate in her arms, Mama told the story. The story Kate had heard many times before. Yet it had never seemed so real.

"Because He loves us, God sent His perfect Son to die on the cross. When you do something wrong, you can say you're sorry. You can ask forgiveness. Jesus *will* forgive you."

Kate looked up as though afraid to believe that was true.

Yet Mama went on. "When you ask Him to be your Savior, He takes away your sin. He saves you from it."

Kate thought about that for a moment. "So I wouldn't be awful?"

"The Bible says you become clean. As clean as new snow."

In a place deep inside, Kate found Mama's words hard to believe. The memory of Tina dangling from the tree wouldn't go away. *Tina could have died because of me. How can God forgive something like that?*

Then Mama noticed Tina sitting cross-legged on the floor. As Mama reached out her free arm, Tina came to her.

"She's all right, Kate," Mama said, seeming to read Kate's thoughts.

When Mama spoke to Tina in Swedish, her voice changed. Kate knew Mama must be telling the little girl not to climb the tree again.

After a time, Kate blew her nose and said quietly, "I'll go back to my room."

"If you want to be alone, Kate," Mama answered. "But not for punishment."

"Not for punishment?" Kate felt surprised by the love in Mama's voice.

"I think you've had your punishment, seeing Tina in that tree. Now let God forgive you."

*God forgive me?* thought Kate. But she was afraid to say it to Mama.

# 13

## The Hiding Place

As Kate looked up, Tina dangled from the tree. Her feet swung wide, searching for a branch. But she found none. Her body trembled. Her hands loosened. She fell through the air, crashing to the ground.

Kate wakened from her nightmare, filled with terror. Reaching out in the darkness, she felt with her hand, searching the bed next to her. At last she found the little girl's arm. Tina slept on.

But Kate's eyes filled with tears. "She's all right!" In her relief Kate spoke aloud, repeating the words over and over.

What if Tina had fallen? The memory of the little girl's danger seemed more real than knowing she was safely asleep in her own bed.

For a long time Kate lay there, her hands still clenched with fear. Then she remembered what Mama said. "Let God forgive you." Instead of pushing away the words, Kate thought about them.

*I did such awful things. But even so, you love me, don't you, Jesus? You love me the way I am.*

*I'm sorry, Jesus. I'm sorry about the wrong things I did. Will you forgive me?*

In that moment there was something Kate knew deep inside. *Yes! I know you will!*

Often before, Kate had heard about God's love and forgiveness. Now that love and forgiveness seemed real. It seemed as though she had opened an early Christmas present.

For a time Kate lay there, thinking about it. Then she dropped off to sleep. When she woke again, Tina was gone. Morning sunlight streamed through the bedroom window. Kate was glad it was Saturday. More than that, she felt good inside for the first time in many days.

That afternoon, soon after Kate returned from her organ lesson, Lars ran in from the mailbox.

"A letter!" he cried. "It's from Papa!"

Kate, Anders, Lars, and Tina gathered around Mama as she settled herself in her favorite chair. Her eyes shone and a slow smile spread across her face as she opened the letter.

It was written in Swedish, and Kate waited for Mama to translate.

"He's well!" she told the children as she read. "He's lonesome for all of us. He found work in a camp close to the railroad." Mama looked up, her face glowing. "If he can, he'll come home for Christmas!"

Lars and Tina cheered, but Anders asked, "Does he say *when* he'll come?"

Mama shook her head, disappointment clouding her eyes. "And he doesn't say he'll come for sure. He says, '*If* I can come.' "

Anders looked as disappointed as Mama. He would be afraid to hope, and Kate knew why.

"Lots of men don't get home for Christmas," he had told Kate once.

"Even if they really want to come?" she asked.

"It's too far to walk when it's real cold. Often there's no other way."

But Kate felt a glimmer of hope. "If he's close to the railroad—" She stopped, knowing how disappointed everyone would be if Papa didn't come.

But Mama spoke Kate's thoughts. "Maybe he can walk to the

railroad and take a train. Maybe he'll leave Dolly and Florie at the camp and come."

"I wish we knew for sure." Lars's voice was small.

"Yah," Mama answered, and Kate felt surprised how often Mama sounded Swedish these days. When married to Kate's Irish daddy, Mama seldom used the Swedish yes.

Now her eyes brightened. "Let's believe Papa will come. Let's get ready for Christmas as though we expect him. If he doesn't come, we'll have Christmas when he does."

They were still talking about Papa's letter when Erik knocked on the door. After they told him the good news, he and Anders went out to the barn. Kate went into the front room to practice her lesson.

Instead of a pipe organ needing to be hand pumped by someone else, Kate had a reed organ. As she pumped the two pedals up and down, the organ filled with air and her mind filled with questions. She still wanted to ask Erik about the day she fell through the ice.

"He's nice," Kate told herself, trying to push aside her memory of the dark, cold water. "He watches out for me." More than once she'd caught Erik looking at her.

But today he still looked worried. Kate knew he must be thinking about the stolen fruit and vegetables.

She touched the ivory keys and started to play. Mr. Peters had given her Christmas carols to practice. Now she had an idea. She could learn "Silent Night" and surprise Papa.

Kate went over the notes for the right hand until she played them without mistakes. She liked the last line especially: "Sleep in heavenly peace."

As Kate practiced the left-hand chords, the boys came in from the barn. Immediately she stopped playing.

"Hey, we want to hear," said Erik.

"Yah, Kate," Anders joined in. He bowed, extending his right hand with a flourish. "Erik, do you know whose pleasure we have the company of keeping?"

Erik grinned, but shook his head.

Anders dropped his voice, sounding formal and adult. "Mr. Lundgren, may I have the pleasure—the pleasure, mind you.

May I have the pleasure of presenting Miss Jenny Lind?"

"You meanie!" Kate blurted out. "I never said I'm Jenny Lind!"

"Excuse me!" Anders cleared his throat.

Throwing back his shoulders, he stood as tall as possible, then lifted his chin. "Correction please!" he announced. "This is *not* Miss Jenny Lind. But listen to the marvelous quality of her notes. She *plays* like Miss Lind *sings*."

As Kate wondered what Erik would think, she felt an embarrassed blush rush into her cheeks. Aloud she sputtered, "Aw, Anders, forget it!"

She stole a quick look in Erik's direction. He was shaking his head at Anders.

Anders paid no attention. Chin still high in the air, he went on. "And one day—one day, mind you, she will travel. She will travel around the world playing the organ."

Kate could stand it no longer. "I hate you, Anders Nordstrom! I hate you!" Spinning on the stool, she turned to the organ and buried her face in her hands.

"Stop it, Anders!" said Erik in a low voice.

But Anders was not to be stopped. "Audiences from one side of the country to another, yea, even from one end of the world to another—"

Suddenly Kate heard a loud thud. Whirling around on the stool, she found the boys wrestling on the floor.

*Erik jumped him!* Kate guessed, filled with glee. "Get him, Erik!" she called out. "Beat him up!"

But just then Mama stood in the doorway. "What in the world!" she exclaimed. "Fighting in the front room! Stop it!"

Immediately the two boys separated. Erik looked as embarrassed as Kate felt when Anders teased.

"I certainly thought you boys knew better than that!" Mama exclaimed. "If you don't have anything more to do, I want you to clean this room for Christmas."

Behind Mama's back, Anders dropped one eyelid in a long, slow wink at Kate. Kate stuck out her tongue. But Erik turned red under Mama's gaze.

Mama had them take all the furniture into the dining room, then said, "Roll up the carpet."

Even Anders moved faster than usual.

Carrying the carpet outside, the boys hung it over the clothes line. Mama supplied a beater and put Anders to work. Each time he hit the rug, clouds of dust rose in the air.

Erik helped Kate sweep the floor, then put down two or three inches of fresh straw. When Mama went out to the kitchen, Erik whispered to Kate, "I didn't mean to make her mad."

Kate giggled. "I've never seen anyone take down Anders."

Erik grinned. "We're a close match."

"You would have won if Mama hadn't stopped you," said Kate.

"You think so?" The grin reached Erik's eyes. Then he sobered. "Sorry, Kate."

"Sorry?" Kate asked.

"About what Anders said."

For the first time Kate wondered how often Erik teased because Anders urged him on. Then she realized something else. "Anders used you as an excuse."

Erik looked relieved. "Glad you feel that way. I wouldn't want Anders teasing *me* about voice lessons."

"You take *voice* lessons?" asked Kate.

Erik nodded, his face flushed. "In exchange for pumping the organ for Mr. Peters. I've never told anyone else."

"Don't worry. I won't tell Anders," Kate promised.

"You won't tell me what?" asked Anders, coming in.

But Kate wouldn't answer, so Anders went back outside. Quickly she asked the question that had bothered her since the day she fell through the ice. "How did you know I needed help?"

"Saw you leave with Stretch," Erik said shortly.

"So you followed us?"

Erik looked embarrassed. "A ways back."

"Why?" asked Kate, though she knew she would have drowned otherwise.

Erik didn't answer right away. When he did, he said, " 'Cause you're just a girl." Then he added, "I don't trust Stretch."

"But you didn't say anything to Teacher. Were you afraid to tell on him?"

"Nope." From the sound of his voice, Kate knew Erik spoke the truth.

"Then why?"

When he spoke, Erik looked embarrassed again. " 'Cause of something Papa says."

"Your papa?"

"Yup. He says, 'Believe in someone 'til they prove you wrong.' "

"So?" Kate wasn't sure what Erik meant.

"So when it comes to Stretch, I always think something bad. I figured he ran away when you needed help. But when I got there, he was already gone. I couldn't prove it."

"And you didn't know 'til I told you?"

"Been wanting to talk to him ever since," answered Erik. "But he hasn't been back to school."

In spite of all that had happened, something in Kate still wanted to defend Stretch. "Why do you always think something bad?"

Erik lowered his voice. "His father cheated my father. Papa couldn't prove it. That's why we had to move to the farm we're on."

When Anders finished pounding the carpet, he and Erik laid it on the clean straw.

Mama supervised. "Just a bit more this way," she said, trying to get it square to the room. At last she was satisfied.

"Now, young men, please move the furniture back." Just then Mama sniffed the air and fled to the kitchen to rescue supper.

The organ was the last piece of furniture to move back. Anders stood on one end and Erik on the other. "Better help him, Kate," Anders teased as he took hold of the handle on his side. "He's not very strong, you know."

As Erik grasped the other handle, he winked at Kate and picked up his end. Coming from the dining room, Anders stumbled and almost fell. The front of the organ tipped, nearly slipping out of his grasp.

Kate ran forward, grabbing below the keyboard. Erik hung

on, and Anders recovered his hold. As he righted his end of the organ, the music rack swung down. A book fell to the floor.

"Put it down!" Anders ordered. He and Erik lowered the organ to the floor. "Whew! That was close."

"Close, all right!" said Kate. "You could have dropped it!" Walking around the organ, she inspected each side. She felt relieved to see it was all right.

As she picked up the book, Kate turned it over. "That's strange!"

"What is?" asked Erik.

"This book. I don't know where it came from."

"It fell when we almost dropped the organ," Erik said.

"But it's not mine."

"Aw, com'on, Kate." Anders sounded impatient. "Who else would it belong to?"

"I mean it!" Kate flipped her black braid over her shoulder, determined that he believe her. "It's *not* my book!"

"Then where would it come from?" As he dropped to the floor to rest, Anders pushed his blond hair from his eyes.

But Kate stood in front of the organ. The music rack still hung down over the keyboard.

Then she noticed something she'd never seen before. Curious, she moved closer. "Hey, look!"

Erik was beside her now, just as interested as Kate. "A secret hiding place!"

# 14

## The Mysterious Message

*A* hiding place, all right!" exclaimed Kate as Anders jumped up to look.

Behind the usual position of the music rack was an opening. Leaning closer, Kate saw a space between the front and back of the organ. The space extended the full width, from side to side.

"A big hiding place," said Kate. "Big enough to hold small books. Must be where this one came from."

"Bet the organist always put *her* music away!"

But Kate paid no attention to Anders. The afternoon light had faded, bringing shadows and making it harder to see. Kate lit a candle and brought it to Erik. "Could you hold this for me?"

Once more, Kate bent down, looking inside the hiding place. Erik held the candle close.

Reaching in, Kate felt her way around the left side of the opening. "Nothing here."

She and Erik traded places, and Kate checked the other side. Again she felt the bottom, then the sides of the small space. Just as she was ready to give up, she felt something. "There!" she exclaimed. "On this side. There's something stuck!"

"Where?" Erik asked, leaning down for a better look.

"Maybe it's a hidden message!" said Kate.

Anders hooted. "Girls and their imagination!"

Kate felt uncomfortable, but she leaned closer, her fingers still feeling the way. In the crack between the bottom and side boards, she felt a paper. Just a small piece of paper.

Then she managed to catch it between her thumb and forefinger. Gently she tugged. It was stuck.

Once more Kate tried, slowly, carefully.

This time the paper slipped out of the crack. Kate held it up to the light.

"What's it say?" asked Erik.

Anders moved closer, looking over Kate's shoulder.

The piece of paper was small, but Kate handed it to Erik. After finding the dead mouse, she didn't want to look at another message.

Slowly Erik read the words aloud:

*on my side;*
*fear:*
*an do to me?*

In that moment Kate's usual curiosity returned. "What do you think it means?" she asked as Erik returned the paper to her. "Is someone in trouble?"

"Could be," he answered. "But if there is, there's someone on that person's side."

"What about the word *fear*?" asked Kate. "And what's that word?" She pointed to the third line. "*An*? What does *an* stand for?"

Anders took the message and held it close to the candle. Carefully he studied the small piece of paper.

After a moment he said, "It's torn." He ran his finger along the left side. "We've got only part of it."

Leaning close, Kate saw he was right. She went back to the organ, looking again in the secret space. Slowly she slid her fingers across the crack from which she'd taken the message. Yet she found nothing more.

"Let me try," suggested Erik.

As Kate held up the candle, he, too, felt his way around the hiding place. His hand also came up empty.

But Erik refused to leave it at that. Carefully moving his fingers across the wood, he touched each panel and bit of carving on the front of the organ. Next he checked wherever pieces of wood were joined together. Finally he studied the outside panel along the right side.

"What're you doing?" asked Kate.

"Wondered if I could take off that panel. But I can't find a way to do it without hurting the wood." Erik walked around to the back, still searching. "Other half of the message must be here somewhere!"

Anders joined him. While Kate held the candle, the two searched every crack and crevice of the organ. But they found no further bits of paper. Finally they had to give up.

As Anders and Erik set the organ along the wall, Kate had another idea. "The book! Maybe there's a name in it!" Pouncing on it, she opened the front cover. Nothing was written there.

It seemed to be a hymnbook, but Kate could not read the words. She turned to Anders. "Is it Swedish?"

As he looked it over, he grinned. "Yah, sure."

He sounded like Papa, and suddenly Kate felt lonesome. Papa would know what to do with the message. She wondered what his lumber camp was like, and how he was doing.

Erik scanned the pages. "They're hymns, Kate, ones we sing in church."

That didn't help Kate much. She still didn't understand the Swedish church services. Just the same, she kept paging through the book, hoping for a clue.

When she reached the end without finding any writing, Kate felt disappointed. Slowly she put down the book.

Something bothered her. "What if the person needs help? Someone in trouble might write a note."

For once Anders was serious. "Hoping that whoever bought the organ would find it."

"When did you get the organ?" asked Erik.

"A few months ago," Kate told him.

Erik looked puzzled. "Something seems strange to me. Why didn't you find the hidden space before?"

"Yah, Kate," Anders drawled. "You certainly should notice things better."

Kate was weary of Anders and his teasing. But Erik seemed not to notice. Going back to the organ, he turned up the music rack. When he set it in place, the rack completely hid the empty space behind.

Then Erik grasped the top of the rack and swung it forward. "Bring the candle!"

As Kate held it up, Erik took a better look. Once more he put the rack back in the position to hold music.

"That's why you didn't notice it, Kate. See how the hinges are hidden? Unless you knew what to look for, you'd never see 'em. Whoever built this organ knew what he was doing!"

Kate felt better then, but something still bothered her. "We don't know how long the note's been there. Did someone write it many years ago? Or just before we got the organ?"

"How old is it?" asked Erik.

"The man we bought it from said 1885."

"Well, let's just ask him!" exclaimed Erik.

"I don't know who he is," answered Kate. "When we went to the fair in Grantsburg, I walked along the street where things were sold. That's when I found the organ."

"So you don't know who sold it?"

Kate shook her head. "Never heard his name."

Erik turned to Anders. "What about you? Were you there?"

"Saw him, that's all," Anders said. "Papa took care of it. I took Kate to see Wildfire so she wouldn't know."

Kate still remembered that important day as if it had happened yesterday. She remembered sitting down and playing the organ, right there along the street. It was exciting to learn she could pick out tunes, even though she'd never had lessons. Now she understood that she had played by ear.

But in that moment she forgot about the people milling around her. Only after she bargained with the man for the organ did she realize Papa and Anders stood behind her. They had heard her play.

Erik turned to Anders. "You must know the man. Your papa knows everyone."

Anders shook his blond head. "Nope. Only time I ever saw him."

"How did he look?" Erik persisted.

"Light brown hair . . ." Anders' voice trailed off as he tried to remember.

Kate recalled more. "Light brown hair, blue eyes, tall. A long beard."

"But around here there's at least a hundred Swedes who look like that!" Erik exclaimed.

Kate knew he was right. "There's only one person who knows who the man is. That's Papa."

"And he's a long way off in a lumber camp up north." Anders sounded grim. "We don't even know if he'll get home for Christmas."

The mysterious message bothered Kate. She couldn't explain why. For some reason she felt it was important, something she needed to know.

Long after Erik went home she thought about the word *an*. What did it mean? Was it just part of a word? Because the paper was torn, it seemed a strong possibility.

The word *fear* bothered Kate even more. Many times she'd been afraid—when lost in the woods, when facing something new. Even more often, she'd felt afraid of what others would think. She didn't like the feeling.

More than once she asked Anders, "What if someone really needs help?"

# 15

## Big Trouble

*T*he next morning Kate studied the face of every man who entered church. Yet none of them reminded her of the person who sold the organ.

"I'll keep looking," she promised herself. And she did. Wherever she went, she watched for a tall man with light brown hair, blue eyes, and a beard.

At the same time Kate and Anders and Erik kept on with another search. Who would take food from a root cellar? They felt sure it would be the same person who stole Josie's steer. If so, where could fruit and vegetables be hidden?

Each time Kate went into the woods, she took a different way, looking. Always looking.

The unusually warm weather lasted three more days. In her free time Kate escaped to the big rock. It became her special place when she wanted to be alone, away from Anders and his teasing.

Picking up fallen branches, she propped them close together around the trunk of a large tree close to the rock. On the side toward the trail, she left space for a door. By crawling in on her hands and knees, Kate had a shelter of her own.

One afternoon late in November, it started to rain. Before long, the rain turned to sleet, coating every tree limb with ice.

During the night the weather changed again. Kate awoke to the sound of windows rattling in the wind. The upstairs bedroom felt even colder than usual, and she snuggled deep under the quilts. In the morning a four-inch blanket of snow covered the ground.

With snow came thoughts of Christmas secrets. Whispers and presents. Baking and making the entire house spotless.

From a trip to Trade Lake, Anders brought home dried cod, and Mama started it soaking in a barrel of lye. Whether Kate liked the smell or not, they'd have lutfisk for Christmas!

Often Kate thought about the presents she'd give. Sometimes she put on an extra sweater and slipped off to her cold bedroom to knit without anyone knowing. Early in the fall she'd hidden away warm mittens for Anders and Lars. Now, after finishing mittens to replace the ones she lost, she was knitting a scarf for Mama.

Each day Kate practiced "Silent Night" to play for Papa if he came home. But what about Tina? What would she like?

While the snow was still new on the ground, Erik skied over. As he waited for Anders and Lars, he called to Kate, "Come with us!"

Kate longed to go along, to ski across the open field in front of the farmhouse, to swoop down the big hill nearby. But she had to tell him, "I don't have any skis."

On a Saturday early in December, Erik returned. For the first time since his family's food was stolen, he didn't look worried at the back of his eyes.

When Kate came to the door, Erik told her, "Brought some skis."

"Skis?" Kate stared at him, not understanding what he meant.

"Yup. Skis. You know, things you put on your feet."

Kate led him into the kitchen, still not sure what he meant. Erik looked half embarrassed, half proud.

"Like 'em?" he asked, carefully leaning the skis against the wall.

"They're beautiful!" exclaimed Kate. "Where'd you get them?"

"Made 'em," said Erik, rubbing the wood instead of looking at Kate. "Made 'em for you."

"For me?" Kate felt dumbfounded at such a gift. Gently, as though the skis would break, she reached out and touched the wood. The bottom sides were smooth with sanding and waxing.

"But how did you do it?" she asked, still unable to believe they were hers.

When Erik grinned, his embarrassment disappeared. "Cut two boards from a birch. Soaked the front ends in water. Kept 'em in a vise 'til the ends stayed bent." He pointed to the front tips that curved upward. "Pretty good, huh?"

He made it sound easy, but Kate knew better. "Pretty *great!*" She knew Erik liked to work with wood, but never dreamed he could do something like this.

"Papa always makes our skis," explained Erik. "Just watched how he did it."

"And the straps?" Kate asked.

"Found a broken piece of harness and cut it in half. Slid it through." He pointed to the opening he had carved in each ski to hold the strap in place. "Hardest thing was finding buckles. They're pretty old. I'll keep looking for better ones in case these don't last."

Kate thought they were the most beautiful skis in the world. "I can't believe they're really for me!"

Erik grinned again as though it were nothing. "Take my word for it."

Kate caught the pride in his face.

Then he asked, "Want to try 'em out?"

As Kate got her coat, Anders came in. Seeing the skis, he asked, "Where'd those come from?"

"They're mine," Kate said proudly.

"Yours? You going to sit or stand on 'em?" Anders laughed.

Refusing to answer such a dumb question, Kate flipped her braid over her shoulder, and the three went outside.

Just beyond the back step the snow was packed, and Kate set down her skis. She felt excited about learning to ski. Often she'd thought how easy it looked.

Quickly Kate slid her boot inside the strap of a ski. As she stepped onto the other ski, it slid out from beneath her. Suddenly she sat down hard.

Anders laughed. "That's all right, Kate!"

In spite of the cold air, Kate felt the hot flush of embarrassment creep into her face. Without saying a word, she got up slowly, rubbing herself where she hurt.

On her second attempt Kate planted her right ski on top of the left. Trying to move the ski, she lost her balance and landed in a heap.

Kate blinked, refusing to let the boys see her cry. As they took off, she followed slowly, feeling awkward. When they reached the big hollow beyond the farmhouse, she watched as they swooped down the steep hill. Skiing around on level ground, she met them on the far side. But gradually it grew easier. Whenever she fell, Kate picked herself up, dusted the snow off her coat and long stockings, and kept going.

From that time on, Kate skied after school whenever she had the chance. Day by day she felt more sure of herself. She still felt scared on the big hills, but she tried them. Sometimes she surprised even herself by standing up all the way to the bottom.

On those afternoons dusk always came too soon for Kate. She wanted to ski longer. Yet after the cold air, the farmhouse reached out with welcome warmth and the aroma of freshly baked bread.

During the long winter evenings, Kate practiced, learning to play "Silent Night." Once when she felt curious, she took out the book that had fallen from the organ. Kate couldn't read the Swedish words, but tried one tune after another. Then she understood why Mr. Peters wanted her to learn to read notes.

One song seemed familiar. Playing the notes for the right hand, she thought about the tune and wondered if they sang it at church. For some reason it reminded her of Tina.

Then Kate remembered the summer before when Mama and Papa Nordstrom were gone. The four children had been in the root cellar, scared about the storm, and Tina started to sing.

"What is it?" Kate had asked, not understanding the Swedish words.

"Children of the Heavenly Father," Lars told her.

Now Kate felt glad Tina had gone to the barn with Anders. "I'll learn the song for her Christmas surprise!" Kate promised herself. "She'll be here even if Papa isn't."

———————

Day after cold day slipped away. Often when Anders, Kate, and Lars came home from school, one of them asked, "Did you hear from Papa?"

Just as often Mama said no, and "It's probably hard to get mail out." Always she tried to smile. Yet as time went on, Mama looked discouraged.

"A neighbor stopped by," she told Kate and Anders in the third week of December. "Mrs. Berglund is sick again. I made meatballs and bread, and I'll send along Christmas cookies."

With the snow too deep for the farm wagon, Anders backed Wildfire between the shafts of a cutter. Its cushions were upholstered in red, and its body painted black with a red pinstripe. With long runners, the cutter slid over snow-covered roads like a large sled with one seat.

Setting the bowl of meatballs on the floor of the cutter, Kate climbed in. Mama handed her a basket with bread and cookies. "They break easily," she warned.

"I'll take good care of them," Kate promised.

Wildfire pawed the ground, anxious to be off. Anders let her go. Soon they left the driveway behind and headed onto the main road. The late afternoon sun cast long blue shadows on the snow.

As the horse trotted along, the bells on her harness jingled. Anders grinned at Kate. He liked to show off Wildfire's good qualities. "Pretty good mare, huh?"

It was a game between them. She knew he really meant to say, "Mighty terrific animal, don't you think?"

And so Kate answered, "Oh, all right."

"Nice black coat," Anders went on, meaning, "Just like satin."

"Well, if you say so," Kate agreed, her voice lukewarm.

"Good high stepper, even in this snow."

"Yup," Kate answered in the casual voice Anders often used.

But today Anders had a new line. "Bet we can get there in record time."

"Bet we can, but we shouldn't," answered Kate, feeling uneasy. She knew how much Anders liked speed. "Too many drifts. Look at them spreading out across the road."

They were passing through an area where the woods had been cleared. As the wind crossed the open fields, it snatched the snow, heaping it up. The drifts angled higher toward the ditch, lower toward the center of the road.

"No problem!" declared Anders. "Wildfire can handle 'em." Lifting the reins, he flicked them across the mare's back. Immediately Wildfire jumped ahead.

"Stop it, Anders!" Kate said immediately. "Stop it right now!"

Anders laughed. "See how Wildfire likes it? She's been penned up too much."

For a moment Kate wondered if he was right. But then they hit their first drift. The cutter tilted slightly, higher on the ditch side. A moment later the cutter dropped down into a dip.

The next drift was bigger. The cutter tilted more, then settled back on its runners.

Anders laughed, but Kate clutched the cookies on her lap. "Slow down, Anders Nordstrom!"

In that moment Wildfire tore into the biggest drift yet. New snow sprayed up against her forelegs. Kate slid into Anders.

"We're gonna tip!" she cried.

In the next instant they did. Anders, then Kate, spilled out in the snow.

Kate found herself face down in a drift. "Now see what you've done!" she sputtered, coming up with a face full of snow.

Anders was also covered from head to foot. He struggled to his feet. "Where's Wildfire?"

Already the mare was down the road, the cutter on its side, dragging behind.

Standing up, Kate brushed herself off, then looked for the basket she'd held on her lap. "Mama's cookies!" Somehow they'd landed beneath Kate.

Every beautiful cookie was crushed to crumbs. All but one loaf of bread was flattened.

"Oh, Anders, how could you!" moaned Kate. "All that good food! All that work!"

Then she saw the meatballs. They, too, were in the snow.

Kate scrambled to pick them up, then knew it was hopeless. The gravy had splattered in every direction. Meat and gravy mingled with snow and dirt.

"Mama's going to feel really bad!" cried Kate as she found the bowl in a drift. But Anders was already far down the road after the mare.

When Kate caught up with them, Anders looked grim. The cutter lay on its side. The reins were tangled in a bush alongside the road. Wildfire stood in a drift, her sides still heaving.

"Told you we'd tip," said Kate, and Anders looked even more angry.

He unhitched the mare, then said, "We've got to turn the cutter up." Anders seemed to bite off every word.

He and Kate got on one side and tried to lift together. It took all their strength, but finally the cutter rocked onto its runners.

Then Anders saw the damage. One of the long poles that hitched the cutter to the horse had split in half. "Broke the right shaft when we tipped," he muttered.

Kate felt sick inside. She wanted to say, "It's all your fault!" Instead she asked, "What do we do?"

For the first time since she'd known him, Anders seemed angry with himself. "Only one thing to do," he answered. "Walk."

"Walk?"

"Yup, walk. And we better get started. Nearest house is a ways down the road."

Leading Wildfire, Anders set out. Kate set the bowl in the cutter, picked up the one good loaf of bread, and followed. By the time they reached a farm, her legs and feet felt numb with cold. But Anders wanted to go on.

"How come?" Kate asked. "I'm frozen!"

"I don't want to stop here." His voice was firm.

"Oh, Anders, why not?" Kate complained.

"Stretch lives here."

"Stretch?" The older boy hadn't been back to school. Kate

hadn't seen him since the ride from Trade Lake. "He'll help you."

Anders shook his head. "I don't want to ask him for help."

"Everyone helps everyone else," Kate argued. "That's the country way."

But Anders would have passed the farm if Kate hadn't insisted they stop.

When they knocked on the door of the house, there was no answer. "See? No one's home anyway," Anders told Kate.

"Maybe they're in the barn," she answered, looking around. The road from which they'd walked ran along one side of the farm. Steep hills rose on the other three sides, leaving the house and barn in a hollow.

By now the sun lay low against the western horizon. Kate knew that light would soon be gone.

As she started toward the barn, Anders dragged his feet. When she found no one there, Kate headed for a small shed. Just as she reached for the handle, the door opened.

Stretch stepped out. Under his curly blond hair his face looked startled. Quickly he reached behind, shut the door, then stood in front of it. "Looking for something?" he asked.

# 16

## Winter Search

*S*urprised, Kate dropped back.

But Anders stepped forward. "Looking for help."

As he told Stretch about the cutter, the older boy's gaze slid sideways. "Sorry, can't help you out." His voice sounded smooth.

"Why not?" asked Kate.

"Can't leave right now."

Kate couldn't understand this boy who had once seemed so friendly. "Why not?" she asked again.

For an instant Stretch seemed to think. "Can't leave my mother alone."

"I could stay with her while you help Anders," Kate said quickly.

The next moment she almost cried out. Anders had stepped on her foot.

As he faced the older boy, Anders seemed amazingly polite. "That's all right, Stretch. Thanks anyway." Anders tugged Kate's arm.

As they started for the road, Stretch shouted after them. "Try Berglunds. He'll help you!"

"Sure!" Anders called back, then kept walking.

Kate was fuming. "How come you stepped on my foot?" she asked when she thought Stretch could no longer hear. "Why'd you grab my arm? At least you could have let us warm up in the house."

Anders was even more cautious. He waited until they reached the road before speaking. "I wanted you out of there."

Kate raised her chin. "You think I can't take care of myself?"

Anders grinned. "Well, sometimes I'm not sure."

In spite of the distance between them and Stretch, Anders lowered his voice again. "He's hiding something. Notice how he shut the door?"

Kate nodded. She had noticed all right. Yet she didn't want to believe Stretch might be doing something wrong.

Inside her mittens she flexed her fingers to warm them. She tried to wiggle her toes, but couldn't feel if they moved.

Anders spoke again. "And you know what he said about his mother? Far as I know, Stretch doesn't have a mother. She died three years ago."

The cold went into Kate's heart.

———————

Still leading Wildfire, Kate and Anders walked on. As they came to knee-high drifts, Anders stopped.

"Let's ride bareback."

"I don't know, Anders." Kate wasn't used to horses and hadn't ridden Wildfire, even with a saddle.

But Anders didn't give Kate a chance to protest. Clasping his hands, he gave her a step up. Then he clutched Wildfire's mane and swung up behind Kate.

In spite of the drifts, they made good time. Kate even enjoyed the ride.

When they reached the Berglund house, a tall man with blue eyes opened the door. His light brown hair had touches of white near the ears.

He invited them into the entryway, but wouldn't let them come any farther. A strong smell of onions filled the house.

"We've got real bad flu here." He tipped his head toward the onions cooking on the wood stove to clean the air. "Can't let you in. But how can I help you?"

When Anders explained that Mama had sent food for Mrs. Berglund, Kate held up the one good loaf of bread.

"I'm her son Henry," the man answered. "Home to help her out. Sorry for this trouble on our account. But I'll tell you what to do."

Leaving Kate and Anders to warm up in the entryway, he disappeared. Soon he returned wearing warm clothes. Picking up an axe, he told them, "I know just the right tree."

Going to the woods that grew close to the side of their house, Mr. Berglund chopped down a sapling. As he cut off the branches, he told them, "That oughta do you."

He returned to the house and found a hatchet, then shaped both ends of the sapling. When he finished, he handed Anders a strong pole that looked exactly right for a shaft. "You might need this hatchet to fix things up. Drop it off next time you come our way, all right? And here's a rope to lash this shaft to the old one."

By the time Kate and Anders reached the cutter again, it was dark. The farm lantern hadn't broken, and Kate lit it while Anders replaced the shaft.

Once they headed toward home, Kate huddled under a heavy horse blanket. She couldn't help thinking about Stretch. Finally she broke the silence. "Remember what he said?"

Anders guessed Kate's thoughts. "Yup. Stretch told us, *'He'll help you.'* "

"And Mrs. Berglund usually lives alone. So Stretch knew her son was home from St. Paul."

"But that's not unusual." For a change it was Anders who defended Stretch. "Everybody knows what their neighbors are doing."

"Even when there's a woods between them?"

"Yup. They depend on each other."

As they turned onto the road to Windy Hill Farm, the moon came up. The large golden ball washed the snow with light.

Again Kate spoke. "You know, there's something that bothers

me about Henry Berglund. Seems like I know him, but I can't figure out where."

Just as they reached the barn, she remembered. "Oh, Anders! That's *him*!"

"That's who?"

"Mrs. Berglund's son, Henry. He's the man who sold the organ!"

"You're sure?"

"Positive!" exclaimed Kate. "Tall with light brown hair. Blue eyes and a beard. That's him, all right. How stupid I am! If only I'd realized it before. I could have asked if he knew anything about the hidden message!"

"We'll go back the first chance we get," promised Anders.

––––––––––

But the next day something important came up. Erik skied over after school. He and Kate and Anders went outside to talk.

Erik had been thinking about something. "Josie's family lost their steer. We lost our fruit and vegetables. Josie's farm and ours are on two sides of the woods. You're on the third side."

"What are you getting at?" asked Anders.

"None of us live far apart."

Then Anders caught on. "So whoever is stealing might know all about us. At least all about where we live."

A scared feeling tightened Kate's stomach. "I don't like that idea."

But Erik went on. "Been thinking about something else. What does that person do with all the food? Eat it? Sell it to someone?"

"If he does sell it, we've got to find it soon," said Anders grimly.

"Before he gets rid of it?" Kate asked.

Erik nodded. "We've got to catch him with the goods. If we don't, you might be the next person he steals from. How long can you keep watching your pig? When's the thief going to find just the right time to grab it?"

Kate didn't like that idea either.

Then Anders thought of something they hadn't tried. "Let's

spread out, all around our farm. Let's look for anything we can find."

"You mean by skiing?" Kate asked.

Anders nodded. "If we go around the drifts, it won't be too deep. Let's each take a direction."

"You can go toward Josie's," Kate answered.

Anders grinned, but all he said was "Yup!"

Erik agreed. "And unless we find something real soon, we'll talk on the way to school tomorrow."

"So what do we look for?" asked Kate.

"Anything that seems strange," Erik told her. "But don't try catching the thief on your own. Come back and tell us."

"Yah, Kate," said Anders. "Remember now."

They divided the area between them, and each set off alone. At first Kate enjoyed skiing. By now she'd gone often enough to feel comfortable with most hills. The day was warm for December, yet cool enough for good skiing.

As she found nothing out of the ordinary, she skied farther and farther from home. She'd never been this way before and liked seeing new hills and farms. Before long, all the markers she knew were far behind.

Finally Kate realized, *I don't know where I am*.

Then she saw the sun sinking toward the western horizon. It gave a sense of direction that would help her get back. But she had to get home before dark.

"Just up this hill," Kate told herself. If she skied back down, it would give a good start toward home.

Reaching the top, Kate looked beyond to a wide valley. Below her lay a house and barn and smaller buildings. Nestled in a hollow, the farm was surrounded on three sides by hills. On the fourth side a road passed the farm.

Just then a boy who sat tall on the seat of a sleigh drove into the yard. Even from a distance, Kate recognized him. She raised her hand to wave and call out.

But in that moment she felt uneasy. Slipping off her skis, she crouched down and peered out from behind a small pine tree.

The boy began throwing branches off the sleigh. Then he

went into the barn, brought out straw, and added it to the layers already in the sleigh.

As he hurried into the house, Kate crawled forward under the tree, trying to see more. Soon the boy came out, carrying a wooden box. Setting it in the sleigh, he returned to the house. Several times he went back and forth, always with more boxes.

Twice he paused and glanced around as though he felt uneasy. Kate crouched lower. With each box the boy added to the sleigh, her curiosity grew. *What's he doing?* It seemed strange that no one helped him. This time of day his father should be home.

At last the boy covered the boxes with quilts and horse blankets. On top of that he placed the long branches he'd taken from the sleigh. Once more he disappeared into the house.

For a time Kate waited. When he didn't return, she decided, "I'll ski down. I'll see what he's hiding in those boxes."

Then she remembered Erik's words. "Don't try to capture the thief on your own."

"Yah, Kate," Anders had said.

A thief? Kate didn't want to call the boy that. She only knew him as Stretch.

While the shadows lengthened across the snow, Kate stayed on the hill, hoping to see more. When she shivered with cold, she remembered her need to get home before dark.

At least she knew where she was. But now that knowledge worried her.

On the way home, Kate thought about Stretch. Was he the one who stole Josie's steer? What did he have in those boxes? She really didn't know anymore, only that Stretch looked guilty. What was he hiding?

With every question Kate felt more upset. Though Stretch was well liked, Anders and Erik and Lars had drawn back, feeling they couldn't trust him.

"Anders warned me," Kate muttered. "But I didn't listen. How could I be so dumb?" The memory of how she had wanted Stretch to like her embarrassed Kate. She had even defended Stretch to Anders. "What will Anders say if I tell him everything?"

As dread knotted her stomach, Kate argued with herself. "I don't have any proof. I'm just guessing. What if I say something, and Stretch's friends find out?" It wasn't hard to guess what they might do if she told on Stretch. Their singsong chant seemed to ring in Kate's ears: "Tattletale, tattletale!"

But then Kate thought of something even worse. *What if I tell and Stretch finds out? Would he try to get even?*

Suddenly Kate felt afraid. Very afraid. She thought about the mysterious message and the word *fear*. That was how she felt.

"I don't need to do a thing," she decided. "I'll just pretend I didn't see Stretch."

# 17

## December Storm

$\mathcal{A}$s the sun slipped behind the far hills, Kate skied into the Windy Hill farmyard. She found Anders in the barn, milking the cows.

"See anything?" she asked before he could ask her.

He shook his head and directed a stream of milk toward one of the cats. "How about you?"

Kate shrugged her shoulders, but didn't look Anders in the face. Leaning her skis against a wall, she dropped down on a mound of straw. The cat settled on the dirt floor to lick the milk off her fur.

After a time Anders asked, "Something wrong?"

"What do you mean?" Kate didn't want to talk. She especially didn't want to tell what she'd seen.

Yet Anders kept on. "You don't act like yourself."

Kate felt surprised that he had noticed. She also felt unwilling to meet his gaze. As the silence lengthened between them, she shivered. "I'm going to the house to warm up."

"Why don't you wait a minute? I'm almost done." Anders hung the pail of milk on a nail, out of reach of the cats.

"I'm cold," she answered, still not looking at him.

His next words sounded totally unlike Anders. "Kate, I know

it must be hard to believe. But I *am* your brother."

"My brother?" Kate laughed, a short brittle laugh that sounded as cold as ice. "Are you really?"

Before she could stop them, tears flooded her eyes and ran down her cheeks. She turned away, not wanting Anders to see her cry, not willing to give him another reason to tease. Everything seemed more than she could bear.

Finally Kate drew a long shuddering breath and looked at Anders. If she didn't know better, she would have thought he seemed embarrassed.

"I mean it, Kate. You can tell me what's wrong."

Kate blew her nose. In that instant she thought of something more than her fear of what Stretch might do. She remembered all the times and ways Anders had helped her. She remembered how good it felt when she and Mama and the Nordstroms became a family, working together.

*But if I tell Anders everything, what will he say?*

In the next instant there was something Kate was sure of. Something that came out of her talk with Mama the day Tina climbed into the tree. Something that came with receiving God's forgiveness. *Anders might tease. But so what? God loves me the way I am.*

The idea was new for Kate, and it gave her courage to begin talking. At first she stumbled, but then her words came faster. To her surprise it was a relief to tell Anders all that had happened.

When she finished, Anders looked at her hard. "Why didn't you tell me you went down to the lake with Stretch?"

"I was afraid of what you'd say."

"How come you were scared to tell me what you just found out?"

"I thought you'd tease 'cause I stuck up for Stretch."

Anders hooted. "You worry about *that*?" But then he said, "Kate, I won't tease you about important things. All right?"

He stretched out his hand and waited for her to shake on it.

When she did, he winked. Kate knew the old Anders was back.

"But the unimportant things—"

Kate withdrew her hand and hit his shoulder. "I know. *You'll* be the one who decides what's important!"

His eyes gleamed with laughter, and Kate knew she'd read his thoughts. She remembered Papa Nordstrom's words: "You'll have to earn your way with Anders."

When she spoke again, Kate sounded like her brother. "Well, then. You better figure out what to do."

"We have to know for sure," Anders told her. "Is Stretch the thief or isn't he?"

Pushing the shock of blond hair out of his eyes, Anders thought for a moment, then went on. "I'll talk to Erik on the way to school tomorrow. You keep Lars and Chrissy busy. If they said anything, it'd get back to Stretch. Somehow we have to figure out how to tell the right grown-up."

"Without letting anyone know we talked," Kate added.

"But how?" Anders looked worried.

They thought about one idea, then another. At last Kate said, "We have to find a way to get to Big Gust."

Since solving the mystery of the disappearing stranger, she and Anders had not seen the seven-and-a-half-foot village marshal. They seldom traveled the eleven long miles into Grantsburg.

"Can he arrest someone out in the country?" Kate asked.

Anders shrugged. "I don't know. There's the county sheriff, Charlie Saunders. Maybe he'd have to come out."

"Big Gust can tell us what to do."

"If we're right about Stretch, we have to be able to prove it," warned Anders.

Kate sighed. "If only I could have seen what was in those boxes."

"Got any ideas?"

Kate shook her head. "All I know is that Stretch didn't want it to freeze. He covered the boxes with quilts and horse blankets."

"So we're back to one problem—proof."

Kate agreed. "Or it's just our word against his."

Anders looked grim. "And we have to find that proof before he gets rid of what he's hiding."

———

During the night a wet snow outlined the dark tree branches with white. When Kate, Anders, and Lars walked to school, the pines looked soft, bending beneath the heavy snow. Kate lingered behind, enjoying the beauty of the woods.

At the fork in the trail they met Erik and his sister. Looking at Kate, Anders tipped his head toward Lars and Chrissy.

When Kate caught up with them, Lars seemed surprised. Kate had barely spoken to him since finding the mouse in her bed.

"Last day of school before getting out for Christmas!" Kate forced herself to sound glad. For the first time in her life, she'd given little thought to vacation. Too many other things had happened.

Chrissy's eyes sparkled with plans for the school party that afternoon.

Lars was looking forward to something else. "Christmas Eve's tomorrow night," he said. But then came the question Kate dreaded. "Will Papa be home for Christmas?"

Mama and Kate and Anders no longer asked that question aloud. They asked it only in their hearts.

*Yes, he'll be here!* Kate wanted to tell Lars. She wished she could make that promise. Instead, she had to say, "I don't know, Lars. I don't know."

Kate ached with the hope that Papa would be home. Her thoughts echoed those of Lars. *Christmas Eve tomorrow night.* She wondered if Papa was somewhere in the cold, walking toward Windy Hill Farm.

In spite of Kate's answer, Lars looked relieved to have her talk to him again. Soon he slipped into his old way of telling her things.

Once Kate glanced over her shoulder. Anders and Erik had dropped back, walking slowly. No doubt Anders was telling him about her discovery. They'd figure out what to do.

But then Kate remembered what Anders said. "We have to be able to prove it. We have to find that proof before Stretch gets rid of it."

Soon after they reached school, the sky grew dark and snow began to fall. By noon that snow blocked out the view of Spirit Lake.

Cold air swept through the knotholes in the floor, and Kate felt the temperature drop. Then the wind came up, swirling snow around the corners of the school.

Often Miss Sundquist walked to the windows and stared at the sky. Finally she went out to stand on the porch. When she returned, she closed the door hard against the wind.

"We won't be able to have our Christmas party," she said, and everyone groaned. "Instead, I'm going to let you out early. Go right home. Don't stop to play on the way."

Kate wasn't sure which she wanted more, the party or leaving school early. At the same time, she felt disappointed. The snow-storm would make it even harder to go to Grantsburg and talk to Big Gust.

As everyone hurried out of school, Kate tucked the long ends of her scarf inside the collar of her coat. Then she followed Anders and Erik down to the creek.

The log was slippery from packed snow, and Kate drew back, fearful of the water rushing beneath. But for once Anders didn't tease. Reaching back to grab her hand, he helped Kate across.

Erik led Chrissy, and Lars made it over on his own. As they climbed the path back of the school, the hill sheltered them. When they neared the top, a cold wind caught their clothing. Even so, the woods offered protection.

Then they reached a field filled with the stumps of recently dropped trees. There the wind howled across the wide open area. Strong gusts picked up new snow, sending it toward them in clouds.

Already, the wind had erased the path they'd packed down walking to and from school. Anders took the lead, breaking the way. Lars went next. Erik dragged his feet to make the path easier for the girls. Kate followed Chrissy.

Here the wind struck her full in the face, and Kate's eyes started to water. The driving snow stung her cheeks. It felt like a thousand needles pricking her skin.

Kate stopped. Unwinding her long scarf, she wrapped it over her forehead, nose, and mouth, leaving only her eyes uncovered.

As she started out again, falling snow blocked her view of the others. In that short time they'd walked on.

For a moment Kate felt panic. Then Erik called. "Come on, Kate! Hurry up!"

"I can't see you!" she called back.

"Keep coming toward my voice," he shouted above the wind. "Follow the footprints."

When she caught up, Erik told her, "Now don't drag."

They plodded on, not wasting the energy to speak. Often Kate saw Erik turn, checking to see that she and Chrissy still walked close behind.

When they entered the woods once more, the wind lessened. Kate felt relieved. Most of the rest of the way would take them through woods. Yet even here the deepening snow made every step difficult.

"It'll keep us home," Kate told herself. "We can't go to Big Gust."

As she felt the disappointment, they reached the fork leading to Erik's farm. Kate wished they could all stay together. Yet there'd be no way to tell Erik's parents where he and Chrissy were if they stayed at Windy Hill Farm.

"Whatever happens, keep moving," Erik told Kate. He seemed much older than his thirteen years.

A moment later, he and Chrissy disappeared in the swirling snow. Kate trudged on, staying close behind Lars. Anders kept the lead, breaking trail.

Suddenly Kate heard a startled cry. Running forward, she found Anders rolling in the snow. "What happened?"

Anders spoke through clenched teeth. "Feels like someone stuck me with a knife."

As he tried to stand up, Kate offered a hand. Anders motioned her away. "I can do it!" Yet he lost his balance and fell back to the ground, groaning.

This time Anders let Kate and Lars help him to a sitting position. Pulling off her mitten, Kate reached forward to feel his ankle.

"Don't touch it!" he exclaimed.

"What happened?" Kate asked again.

"Couldn't see the path." Anders gritted his teeth.

Then Kate saw two small logs just off the trail. They lay close together, partly covered by ice and snow. Anders must have slipped off the first icy log, twisting his foot between that and the next.

"What should I do?" Kate wanted to know.

But Lars surprised her by asking Anders, "Can you wiggle your toes?"

Anders winced with the effort, but nodded. Even in the swirling snow, Kate saw the pain in his eyes.

Her stomach felt empty, and she knew what it was: fear all the way through. That day when she fell through the ice, Anders and Erik had carried her most of the way to school. Kate knew she and Lars weren't strong enough for that.

"Can you possibly walk?" she asked Anders.

He shrugged, as though knowing he didn't have any choice.

Again Lars took over. "Gotta fix his boot first."

Again Kate looked at him as if to ask, "Do you know what you're talking about?"

Lars seemed to guess her thoughts. "Papa got hurt in the woods once. He told me what to do."

Anders was wearing Papa's old work boots. Lars knelt in the snow in front of Anders, unlaced the boot on the injured foot, then loosened it. Already the ankle looked swollen.

Anders bit his lip, as though fighting the pain. His eyes were wet with tears.

*I've never seen Anders cry before,* Kate thought. Once Kate would have teased him. Instead, she felt even more scared.

"Put your arms around our shoulders," she told him. She and Lars pulled Anders to a standing position.

"We'll make it," she said, trying to sound confident. But her words seemed to vanish into the snowy air.

Anders stepped gingerly on his bad foot, putting as much weight as possible on his good one. As he limped along, Kate saw him bite his lip against the pain.

He was so much taller and heavier that Kate soon felt exhausted. *What can we do?* she wondered, feeling desperate. *How can we get him home?*

In the next moment Anders stumbled and fell forward.

# 18

## *Whistle in the Dark*

*J*ust in time Kate and Lars caught Anders.

His face looked gray. Beads of perspiration dotted his upper lip.

"What can we do?" This time Kate spoke aloud. When neither Anders nor Lars answered, the words set up a rhythm in her mind.

Then Kate remembered the shelter she'd built that fall. She'd gone there when she wanted to be alone, away from Anders and Lars and their teasing.

The big rock and the shelter weren't far away. There Anders could be out of the wind while she went for help. Yet a part of Kate held out. *It wouldn't be my secret anymore.*

A gust of wind swept down the path, pushing against them. With it came the pain of all the times and ways Anders had teased her. "And Lars isn't any better," Kate told herself, remembering the mouse in her bed.

Her shoulder ached from the weight of supporting Anders. His breathing sounded labored.

"You're strong," she told Anders. "You can do it."

But Anders stumbled again. Never before had Kate seen him so helpless.

Lars stopped. "He can't get all the way home. Not in this storm."

Kate knew Lars was right. As clearly as if Anders had spoken aloud, she remembered his words: "Kate, I'm your brother."

They stood close to the large oak and the clump of birch marking the way to her shelter. "This way," she said, tipping her head to the left of the path.

In a few minutes, they reached the big rock and the shelter Kate had built. The wet snow of the night before still clung to the branches, filling the cracks.

"Hold Anders," she said to Lars.

Kneeling at the doorway, Kate crawled inside. At once she felt the difference. Out of the wind it was warmer. The snow on the branches offered even more protection.

Half pulling, half dragging, they helped Anders into the shelter. Lars took off his brother's boot and pushed snow under the bad leg, propping it up.

Kate drew off her coat, then a sweater. When she wrapped the sweater around his foot, Anders flinched. Even in the half light, his ankle looked more swollen.

"Make sure he doesn't leave," Kate told Lars as she slipped back into her coat. If Anders started out again, she might not find them.

"Why don't you stay too?" Lars asked.

"Maybe I should," Kate answered, looking at Anders. For the first time since she'd known Anders, he was unable to help her decide.

Then Kate remembered Mama. She would be worried, wondering where they were. As Anders trembled with pain, Kate made up her mind. "Might be an all-night snow."

"I'll go," offered Lars.

"We need Wildfire," said Kate. "You've never hitched her up, have you?" Lars was even shorter than Kate. Once more, she wrapped the long scarf around her face.

"Don't stop," Lars said, echoing Eric's words. "Keep moving no matter what."

Outside the shelter, Kate felt the wind again. Close by, the trees thinned out and a steep bank dropped away to Rice Lake.

Kate turned the opposite direction and headed back to the trail.

Soon after coming to Windy Hill Farm, she had lost her way in the woods. Using the sun, she had headed in one direction. But today there was no sun, only steadily falling snow.

When Kate reached the clump of birch and the tall oak that were her markers, she turned onto the path. Snow hid the trail packed down by their daily walks, but Kate watched for the opening between the trees.

"Where are you, Papa?" she muttered as she plodded on. "Are you out in this too?"

After walking for some time, Kate came to the part of the trail edging Rice Lake. Once again the full force of the wind struck her. She gasped, and bent her head low.

Turning her back to the wind, Kate looked around now and then to keep her bearings. As she trudged on, walking backward, the banks of snow looked inviting—as inviting as a large soft bed.

*I'm tired*, Kate thought, wanting to lie down.

"Keep moving, no matter what," Eric had said.

*I'll just rest for a minute.*

"Don't stop," Lars had told her.

Now Kate understood why. She wanted only to sleep.

She faced into the wind, and at last felt a rise beneath her feet. She'd passed the spring along the wagon track without knowing it. Step-by-weary-step, Kate climbed the steep hill near the farmhouse. At the top she saw a faint glow. Mama had a candle in the window!

Kate headed for the light. Pushing open the kitchen door, she stumbled in.

"Kate!" exclaimed Mama. She hugged Kate tight, snowy coat and all.

Tina's blue eyes were wide, but it was Mama who asked, "Where are Anders and Lars?"

As Kate told her, Mama exclaimed, "Oh, Kate! I wish you could stay here. I wish Papa was here to go." Moving quickly to the cookstove, she set a kettle over the firebox to make cocoa.

Kate shed her coat and put on a warm dry sweater. "I wish Papa was here too," she said, her voice as small as she felt. "But

Anders showed me what to do with Wildfire."

She caught the surprise on Mama's face. As quickly as it came, it disappeared.

Kate pulled on her coat once more and headed out to the barn, wondering if she could remember all that Anders had taught her about handling a horse. Holding the bridle, she entered Wildfire's stall.

"Get over, girl," she told the mare. But her voice came out squeaky and small. Wildfire didn't move.

"Get over," Kate said again, sounding as bossy as she could.

This time Wildfire moved. Kate pulled herself to the top of the feed trough. There she slipped off the halter and held up the bridle.

Her hands shook as she felt along Wildfire's jawline for the place to open her mouth. Carefully she slipped in the bit.

Next came the harness, belly strap, and breast collar. Kate fumbled as she checked the straps and buckles. Finally she picked up the farm lantern and led Wildfire out of the barn.

As she backed the mare between the shafts of the cutter, Kate held her breath. What if Wildfire decided to bolt? Kate knew she couldn't hold her the way Anders did.

Quickly Kate took the lead rope and tied it to a rail. Still talking to the mare, Kate buckled her in.

It seemed forever before she had everything right. At last she lit the lantern, set it in the cutter, and climbed in. *I'm ready—or I think I am!*

At the house, Mama hurried out, handing up a heavy basket. She'd filled jars with cocoa, wrapping them to stay warm. "I'll be praying for you!" she called out above the wind, then stepped away from the runners.

Reins in one hand, Kate waved and clucked the horse. Then she guessed the worry Mama must feel. Turning back, Kate threw her a kiss.

For just a moment Mama smiled. The concern in her eyes disappeared. Before the snow swallowed her up, Mama blew a kiss back.

Kate felt warm inside. She remembered to shift a rein to the other hand as she thought about her first year of school. She'd been afraid to go off on her own to a big new world.

At first Mama walked with her to the Minneapolis school. Then Mama asked older children to take her. When Kate still felt afraid, Mama started a game. Standing inside a front window, she waved. Kate waved back. Kate blew a kiss, and Mama returned it.

The old signal still worked. Now it meant more. In spite of all that had happened, she had no doubt that Mama loved her.

At the bottom of the steep hill, Kate whistled. Lutfisk bounded up, and Kate was glad she'd learned how to call him. She flicked the reins and Wildfire picked up her pace.

By now the December afternoon had faded into dusk. Along Rice Lake the wind had blown the path clean. In other places the snow lay in deep drifts.

Near the edge of the woods, one of these drifts reached the mare's chest. Wildfire hesitated, and Kate shouted, "Come on, girl. Go on through!"

Snow sprayed up as Wildfire plunged ahead. The cutter tilted, then settled back on its runners. Choking down her fear, Kate cried out, "That-a-girl! Keep it up!"

The mare's ears twitched and turned toward the sound of Kate's voice. "Good girl!"

As they entered the woods, the dusk deepened. Kate's hands tensed. Yet she urged the horse on, trying to keep her on the packed trail now hidden by new snow.

Once Wildfire stepped off the trail and staggered into deep snow. For a moment she stood there, pawing the ground. Finding the path again, she strained against the harness.

When dusk changed to night, Kate pulled on the reins for Wildfire to stop. Grasping the long metal handle, Kate held up the farm lantern. As it swung in the wind, she picked out trees on either side of the trail. None of them seemed familiar.

A gust of wind swooped down. The flame flickered but held.

Setting the lantern by her feet, Kate picked up the reins and flicked them across Wildfire's back A few minutes later Kate stopped again to hold up the lantern. This time she felt even more confused. "Where are we?" she muttered, unable to recognize the trees.

In that moment the lantern flickered and died. The darkness of deep woods closed in around Kate as she realized the awful truth—she hadn't filled the lantern with kerosene!

Yet she had no choice but to keep on. As Wildfire moved ahead, Lutfisk barked. Kate peered into the night. No matter how hard she looked, she couldn't find the tall oak and the clump of birch.

The fear within her growing, Kate called out. "Anders! Lars!" But the wind threw back her voice. No one could possibly hear.

Switching both reins into one hand, Kate pulled off her mitten. With her thumb and finger between her lips, she blew hard. Her shrill whistle pierced the air.

For a moment Kate listened. Lutfisk yipped and ran alongside the cutter. But there came no other sound.

Kate's fear changed to panic. Once more she blew hard. Listening, she wondered if she heard a response.

When she whistled a third time, an answering whistle pierced the night. Lutfisk broke away and disappeared in the darkness.

*They're behind me!*

Kate whistled still again. When she heard the answer, she felt sure. "I went too far!" she muttered. "I've gone past them!"

The trail was too narrow to turn the cutter. Wildfire plodded on as Kate heard yet another whistle. Then it fell away.

At last the dim outline of trees disappeared from either side of the path. Reaching the field, Kate pulled on the reins. She turned Wildfire, and they reentered the woods.

As they drove through the darkness, Kate whistled often. Finally she heard an answer. Then the clump of white birch loomed out of the darkness.

Stopping Wildfire, Kate jumped down and tied the mare to a tree. Carrying Mama's basket of hot cocoa, Kate headed off the path.

Now she had a new fear. *What if I miss the shelter? I'd fall over the steep bank next to it!*

# 19

## The Flickering Candle

*K*ate stood still. Once again she pulled off her mitten and whistled. From the swirling snow she heard the response—a long, clear answer.

Out of the darkness Lutfisk hurled himself toward Kate. When she reached down to pet him, he jumped up and barked. Then he darted away. A short distance off, he stopped, waiting for Kate to follow.

She reached him, and he darted away again. Each time the dog left her, he stayed close enough for Kate to see.

Before long she heard Lars shout, "Kate, over here!" Lutfisk had brought her to the shelter.

Reaching the door, Kate tumbled inside. After the darkness and snow, the shelter seemed warm and safe.

They warmed up on cocoa; then Kate and Lars helped Anders out of the shelter. His arms once more around their shoulders, the three started out. Soon they reached the cutter safely.

As they helped Anders in, he bumped his leg and moaned. Once settled, he spoke between clenched teeth. "Give Wildfire her head. She'll find her way home."

As Kate flicked the reins, Wildfire leaped out. The going was slow as the mare worked through the drifts. Finally they reached the top of the hill and the farmhouse. This time Mama had three candles in the window.

When they came into the kitchen, Kate saw Anders' face. In the light of the kerosene lamp his lips looked white, his eyes glazed with pain. Mama had a bed of blankets ready for him on the floor near the wood stove.

---

During the night the wind died down. In the early morning sunlight, the snow glistened—white and beautiful. Kate remembered Mama's words: "When Jesus forgives, you become clean. Clean as new snow."

This morning Kate believed those words. She felt peaceful inside. "Christmas Eve tonight!" she told herself. She dared to hope. "Maybe Papa came home during the storm!"

But then Kate remembered Stretch. She remembered how she and Erik and Anders planned to go to Big Gust. And she remembered how Anders got hurt.

Down in the kitchen, Kate didn't need to ask. Tina and Mama worked quietly. Lars was out milking the cows. Papa hadn't come during the night.

Still lying near the wood stove in the dining room, Anders looked pale. He whispered to Kate. "I don't know if I had a nightmare or if it was real. Go check on the pig."

Outside, the snow had blown against the summer kitchen, heaping it in high drifts. Yet in front of the door, the snow was less than a foot deep. Looking at it, Kate felt afraid.

Quickly she shoveled away enough snow to open the door. Inside, the little house was icy cold. But Kate looked for only one thing.

The top of the cookstove was bare. The pig was gone!

Kate's fear changed to anger. She felt angry at whoever stole Josie's steer. Angry at the person who took raspberries and blueberries and carrots and potatoes from Erik's cellar. Angry at the thief who stole their pig.

Kate wanted to pound her fist on the top of the cookstove. Then she noticed. One round stove lid was missing.

That made Kate even more angry. Without that lid, the stove

was useless. If the family started a fire, the room would fill with smoke.

Hurrying back to the house, Kate told Anders, Mama, and Tina the bad news. "The pig's gone!"

Tina's eyes grew wide, and Mama threw up her hands. "In the midst of that storm, someone came?"

Angrily Anders slammed one fist into another. But when he tried to stand up, he groaned.

Lars came in and found out about the pig. He looked just as upset.

As Mama filled plates with eggs and warm brown bread, Anders whispered to Kate. "We've gotta get to Stretch."

"While we can still prove it!" Kate exclaimed in a low voice. "But how?"

During breakfast Mama had more than the pig on her mind. "Christmas or no Christmas, Anders has to see the doctor in Grantsburg. His ankle is even more swollen this morning. I can't tell if it's sprained or broken. It might need to be set."

"I'll take him, Mama," Kate said quickly.

"You, Kate? No, absolutely not."

"I can do it, Mama."

"Eleven miles? You can't do it alone."

"I'm sure I can, Mama," said Kate, even though she felt nervous about it.

Mama sighed. "Well, I guess you're right. But you'd have to take the sleigh so Anders can lie down."

"Sleigh's too heavy for Wildfire alone," Anders told her. "At least with these drifts."

Kate turned to him, surprised that Anders would object to going to Grantsburg.

Anders went on. "Get Erik. See if he can drive their team of horses."

By the time Lars and Erik returned with Lundgrens' horses, Mama had sandwiches and cocoa ready.

Erik looked grim as he checked out the freezing-cold summer kitchen. "Did you see you're also missing a stove lid?"

He spread heavy blankets in the sleigh for Anders. Inside the blankets, he put bricks Mama had warmed and wrapped in burlap. He and Kate helped Anders in, being as careful as they could. Even so, Anders winced with pain.

As they started out, the sleigh bells jingled bright and clear in the winter air. Yet Erik talked only about the pig. "No footprints in the snow."

"Must have been some," answered Kate. "But the wind covered them." For a moment she thought about it. "Maybe that's why he came last night."

"Pretty smart thief." Erik sounded angry. "We haven't got much time."

Kate knew he was right. "If he cuts up the pig, we won't be able to recognize it."

As they reached the main road, the team picked up speed. Yet the going was slow, and the drifts large.

With each delay Kate grew more impatient. "Even if we get Big Gust, how can we prove the pig is ours?" she asked. And something else bothered her. "I keep thinking about that hidden message. If the organ was Mrs. Berglund's, *and* if she wrote the message, do you think she's still afraid?"

"Could be, living alone," Erik answered.

Anders disagreed, calling out from behind them. "She *wants* to stay on her farm. Even though she lives alone."

Kate wasn't satisfied with that answer. "Then what would make her afraid? We still haven't figured out what *an* means."

"An, an, an." Erik repeated the syllable to himself. "What would *an* do to her?"

For a time they drove in silence. Suddenly Anders shouted, "Man! The word is *man!*"

Erik grinned and looked back. "For someone with a bum ankle, you're doing all right!"

Kate had another thought. "Or it could be *woman*."

"Could be either," Erik agreed as the sleigh plowed into another bank of snow.

Anders moaned. "Can we stop somewhere? Every time we hit a drift, my ankle hurts worse."

"Let's stop at Berglunds' and warm up," suggested Kate. "We need to return their hatchet. And I want to ask about the message."

When they reached the house, Henry Berglund opened the door. Mrs. Berglund was up and around again, and she insisted on feeding them.

"Get me the milk, will you, Kate?" she asked as her son and Erik helped Anders into the house.

Kate lit a candle and pulled up the trapdoor. Step by step she descended into the darkness. This time she cupped her hand around the flame, shielding it from blowing out. Yet as she reached the bottom of the steps, the candle burned steady, the flame straight in the air.

Kate saw the milk on a ledge near the stairs. She picked it up, then set it back down. Why was there a breeze before and not today? Why didn't the candle flicker out?

Holding it out in front of her, Kate looked around. This time she felt determined to see all of the cellar.

The earth basement was small. Kate moved closer to the boarded-off section she'd seen last time. Spotting a door, she opened it. Canning jars and squash filled several shelves.

Nearby were large bins of potatoes and bushel baskets with dirt. Kate knew those baskets probably held carrots stored for winter.

Disappointed, she continued to search. *There must be more.* What would cause a breeze strong enough to blow out a flame?

Circling the room, Kate held her candle high. In the wall opposite the steps leading to the kitchen she discovered another door. On either side, wide ledges were dug into the earth wall.

"Kate!" Mrs. Berglund called down. "Having trouble?"

"Be right there!" Kate shouted back. Moving closer to one of the ledges, she peered into the area lit by the candle. This time she saw something far back on the ledge. Fruit jars. Jars filled with blueberries, raspberries, and strawberries.

Swinging around, Kate looked at the other ledge. A number of bushel baskets stood there. They, too, were set far back, almost out of sight.

Between these ledges was the door she'd seen, and Kate opened it. On the other side, steps led upward. Steps covered at the top by double doors slanted over the opening. "That's it!" Kate exclaimed. If the doors were left open even a little, it would cause a draft.

Closing the inner door, Kate went back to the milk. Just then Mrs. Berglund called again.

"Coming!" Kate shouted, and hurried up the steps.

In the kitchen she quickly glanced around. One window looked out on the slanted boards of the double doors to the cellar. Beyond, the backyard stretched away to nearby woods.

Kate set down the milk near a tall cupboard. She started to turn away, then noticed something. A piece of embroidered cloth hung on the wall.

As she stood on tiptoe to read the words, Kate barely breathed. Filled with excitement, she flipped her long black braid over her shoulder.

This was something Anders and Erik had to see!

# 20

## Big Gust Anderson

$C$ome, come," called Mrs. Berglund before Kate could get the boys. "You still have a long ride ahead of you."

Leaning against Erik, Anders lowered himself into a chair next to the table.

"Christmas Eve tonight," said Henry Berglund after the prayer. "Bad time for you to get hurt, Anders."

Anders agreed. His face looked white and he winced whenever he had to move his ankle. Yet in spite of his misery, he winked at Kate as though to say, "Get talking!"

Kate didn't waste a minute. "Mrs. Berglund, did you ever have your own organ?"

The old woman smiled. "Yah."

Kate turned to the woman's son. "Did you sell that organ last summer?"

"At the street fair in Grantsburg. When they had the county fair."

As she looked back to Mrs. Berglund, Kate's excitement grew. "I think I have your organ."

"Yah? How does it look?"

When Kate described her organ, Mrs. Berglund nodded. "Yah, that's mine all right."

"Then I have a book you left in it."

"Good. I left it for you."

"For me?"

"I hoped the one who got the organ would use it."

"Oh, I am!" Kate exclaimed, and told her about "Children of the Heavenly Father."

But Kate really wanted to ask about the hidden message. More than once, she and Anders and Erik had searched the organ, trying to find the other half of the paper.

"We found part of a message in a crack," said Kate.

"And what did it say?" Mrs. Berglund's eyes twinkled as though she already knew.

"Do you mind if I write it out?" Kate had spied a bottle of ink and a pen on a nearby shelf.

Taking the pen, Kate dipped it in the ink. When she finished, the words said:

*On my side;*
*fear:*
*an do to me?*

Mrs. Berglund smiled. "It's my favorite verse."

"A Bible verse?"

She nodded. "Psalm 118, verse 6."

"And you put it in my organ? I mean, *your* organ?"

"For many years I had it on the music rack," Mrs. Berglund explained. "I wanted to see it there. When Henry took the organ to town, I put the message inside. It must have slipped down in the crack."

"But what does the rest of it say?" Anders sounded impatient.

Now Kate was enjoying herself. She leaned forward and wrote again. When she sat back, Erik jumped up to read the words aloud:

The Lord *is* on my side;
I will not fear:
What can man do to me?

Anders looked puzzled. "Kate, how did you know?" he asked.

"We should get it for Anders," answered Mrs. Berglund.

Her son went to the corner of the kitchen. Coming back, he held up the piece of embroidered cloth.

But Kate had another question. "Were you afraid?" she asked Mrs. Berglund.

Below Mrs. Berglund's faded blue eyes, her smile was gentle. "Yah, I was often afraid."

"Why?" Kate asked again.

"When I played the organ for other people, I was afraid I'd make mistakes. I was afraid of what people would think."

"Did the verse help?"

"Yah, certainly. I always said it to myself. Before I played, I asked the Lord to help me."

"And He did?" Kate needed to know.

"He always did. He still does when I'm afraid. If I hear a strange noise at night, I say that verse to myself."

"Have you heard strange noises lately?" Kate asked quickly, as she guessed what the answer might be.

"Well, now that you mention it, I heard noises a few nights ago, coming from the back of the house. A wagon track goes through the woods there. But it was dark. I couldn't see anything."

Kate turned to Henry Berglund. "Were you here?"

He shook his head. "I was gone overnight. First I've heard about the noises."

———————

On the way to Grantsburg, Kate told Erik and Anders about the cellar. "Why would there be potatoes in *two* places? And canning jars in *two* places?"

Erik's eyes gleamed.

"And why would there be a draft one day and not another?" Kate continued. "Unless doors were open?"

Erik's grin told Kate they were both thinking the same thing.

Anders spoke up from the back of the sleigh. "You know, Kate, for a girl, you're pretty smart." He sounded surprisingly normal.

For once Kate didn't mind his teasing. But then her fear returned. "If it *is* Stretch, what's he going to think if we're the ones turning him in?"

"Now, that's where you *aren't* smart," said Anders.

"If we don't say something, who will?" asked Erik. "He'll keep stealing the rest of his life."

When they reached Grantsburg, Erik went to find Big Gust. Kate stayed with Anders at the doctor's. It was a bad sprain, not a break. The doctor gave Anders crutches and told him to stay off the ankle.

A short time later, Erik returned with the village marshal. After not seeing the big Swede for a time, Kate again felt surprised at his size.

She knew Big Gust was 7 1/2 feet tall, weighed 360 pounds, and wore size 18 boots.

Beneath his moustache, his smile was enormous. When he stretched down his hand to say hello, Kate saw the kindness in his eyes.

"Sheriff Saunders is gone," Erik explained. "But Big Gust's sister lives out our way, near little Wood Lake. He was just ready to leave and visit her for Christmas."

All of them went out to Erik's sleigh, with Anders limping along on his crutches. As he dragged behind, Big Gust turned back. He bent down and picked Anders up.

"Hey, what are you doing?" Anders looked embarrassed, but the marshal set him in the sleigh as gently as if he were a basket of eggs.

Erik grinned at Kate. For a giant known to pick up two men at one time, Anders offered no problem at all.

Big Gust settled himself on the seat and took up the reins. There was just enough room for Erik and Kate to squeeze in next to him, one on either side.

In spite of the cold, Big Gust's coonskin coat hung open. Underneath, he wore his marshal's uniform, a long blue coat with gold buttons down the front. When the coonskin coat swung back, Kate saw the silver star on his chest.

Yet as they headed out of Grantsburg, Kate had to fight down her fear. *What if Stretch finds out I'm the one who told?*

Driving back over the snowy roads, Big Gust told them stories about his boyhood in Sweden. As he talked, Kate felt better.

Each time she wondered what Stretch would think, she repeated Mrs. Berglund's verse to herself. "The Lord *is* on my side; I will not fear: What can man do to me?"

In spite of what Erik had said about the thefts, Big Gust was in good humor. More than once, he reached inside his large pockets.

Kate had heard he always carried candy for the children of Grantsburg, but she'd never seen it before. Now Big Gust drew peanuts in the shell from one pocket, a bag of Christmas candy from another.

"We'll stop at Berglunds' first," he told them.

When they reached the house, the marshal had to stoop down to get through the door. While Anders warmed up in the kitchen, Kate, Erik, and Big Gust followed Henry Berglund into the cellar. There the tall Swede had to crouch on the dirt floor to avoid bumping the ceiling.

Seeing the extra food, Mr. Berglund shook his head. "Someone must have brought it through the outside door. After I take in the potatoes, I cover that door with snow. This year I haven't gotten around to it."

Erik was excited. "Looks like our canning jars!" The bushel baskets with carrots, potatoes, and squash also seemed to be theirs. "And everything looks all right!" It seemed that nothing had frozen.

Kate had an idea. "Erik, did you say a jar was broken? Can you tell if one is missing?"

"Probably," answered Erik. "Mama told me how many she canned of each kind."

They separated the strawberries, blueberries, and raspberries into three groups and started counting.

"They're all here except one blueberry!" Erik told them.

When they left, Big Gust took the wagon track back of the house through the woods. As they drove, Kate felt uncomfortable, wondering if this was the way Stretch had gone.

Soon Big Gust stopped the sleigh in a pine grove, out of sight of Stretch's house. "You stay here," he said. "I'll go by myself."

Kate felt relieved. She was safe. Stretch wouldn't know she'd told the others about him.

The sun was edging down toward the horizon when Big Gust returned. "I found Stretch," he said. "And I found a pig that might be yours."

"Great!" exclaimed Anders.

But Big Gust's face was grim. "Stretch says the pig belongs to him."

Kate looked at Anders, and Anders looked at Erik. It was Anders who spoke. "That's just what we were afraid of. We can't prove a thing."

Big Gust shook his head. "Then I can't do a thing. Not without proof."

As the marshal sat down on the sleigh, Anders groaned. But Kate and Erik looked at one another. In that moment they remembered something.

"The cookstove!" Kate exclaimed.

In his excitement Erik laughed. "The lid was gone!"

"What're you talking about?" asked Anders.

Erik turned to Big Gust. "Did you happen to turn the pig over?"

The big man shook his head.

"Then we've got proof!" cried Kate.

In low voices, they explained to Big Gust, and he grinned.

Forgetting about what Stretch might think of her, Kate jumped down from the sleigh and hurried toward the house.

# 21

---

## *Christmas Morning*

As Kate headed through the pines, Erik and Big Gust followed. Anders limped along on crutches, unable to make much progress through the snow.

Big Gust looked around and went back. With one easy swoop he picked up Anders. Again Anders looked embarrassed. At the same time he seemed grateful for the help.

To the village marshal Anders seemed to weigh nothing at all. Big Gust stretched out his long legs, moving without effort through the deep drifts.

Kate went straight for the small building where she and Anders had found Stretch before. When she pounded on the door, Stretch came out.

He grinned at her, and Kate remembered why she thought he was nice. Yet now that idea made her uncomfortable.

Then Stretch saw Big Gust, Anders, and Erik. The grin disappeared as though a mask slid over the boy's face.

"We want to take another look at the pig," the marshal told Stretch.

It took a moment for Kate's eyes to adjust to the dim light of the shed. Over in one corner was a wooden table. A frozen pig lay upon it, and Kate knew it was theirs.

"It's mine, I tell you," Stretch told Big Gust. "How come you're picking on me?"

The marshal seemed to fill the small shed. "Let's have a better look. What would you say if there was a stove lid frozen to the pig?"

Acting as if he didn't have a care in the world, Stretch walked to the table. Yet Kate saw the side of his face twitch.

Then Big Gust turned the pig over. Frozen to the bottom side was a cookstove lid!

Stretch's eyes flickered. Quickly he turned away, but not before Kate saw him bite his lip.

One moment Kate felt good. They had the proof they needed. The next moment she felt sick. As she glanced at Erik and Anders, Kate guessed they felt the same way.

She almost hated to ask Stretch more. "Your blue hand? Did you break a jar of Erik's blueberries?"

For a long moment Stretch hesitated. Finally he nodded.

"And you carried the jars in boxes and hid them in Berglunds' cellar?" Kate continued.

Stretch looked startled, as though wondering how she knew. Slowly he nodded again.

Anders had his own questions, and he was angry. "Josie's steer? Where is it?"

Stretch's shoulders slumped as he seemed to give up. "I took it where no one knew me. I sold it."

"Why, Stretch?" Big Gust's voice sounded as strong as iron, yet sad.

Stretch's face still seemed a mask, frozen like the pig. When he remained silent, Big Gust asked again. "Why did you do it?"

Kate felt surprised that a man so big could sound so kind.

Stretch must have heard the kindness too. His mask cracked. He looked at Kate, then away. When he spoke, he pushed the words out between his teeth. "I was hungry."

"You were *hungry*?" asked Big Gust. "A boy in northwest Wisconsin is hungry? I can't believe my ears!"

"At first I was hungry." Now Stretch was looking at the dirt floor. "Then I learned I could sell things to buy what I wanted."

"But why?" Kate felt numb, as though she wasn't really hearing Stretch.

Again he looked at Kate, then away. He spoke so quietly she could barely hear. "After Ma died, Pa started drinking. Every year he drank more. This fall he sold the cows. He sold the harvest. All he kept were the two horses."

They went to the house then. Big Gust tried to help Anders, but Anders shook his head.

"Not now!" he exclaimed, looking toward Stretch as though unwilling to be carried in front of him. Yet by the time Anders hobbled through the snow on crutches, he seemed to have difficulty moving another step.

The house was cold, and the supply of wood short, but Erik started a fire. Pulling up chairs, they huddled close.

Stretch told them more. "Pa and I had terrible fights. One night when he fell asleep, I took the money he got from selling everything. I knew he'd drink it up, so I hid it. The next day when I came home from school, Pa was gone. The place I hid the money was empty."

"Where is he now?" asked Big Gust.

Stretch shrugged his shoulders. "I don't know. I haven't seen him for a couple months."

"You've been living here all alone?" Anders asked, his voice low. "And no one knew?"

"Pa always kept to himself," explained Stretch. "Wasn't very neighborly. In winter we're always alone."

"Why didn't you tell us?" Anders asked.

Stretch looked embarrassed. "I didn't want you to know. I was scared of what you'd think of my family."

"So you just dropped out of school?"

Stretch nodded, but he didn't look at Anders.

"And what about Kate?" asked Erik. "How come you left when she fell through the ice?"

Stretch turned to her, his eyes strangely moist. "I'm sorry, Kate. I was so scared that I ran away."

Anger flooded Kate's heart. "I could have drowned!"

Stretch looked as though she had slapped him. In spite of his height, he seemed small as he slumped in his chair.

Watching him, Kate remembered what she'd learned from Mama. She drew a deep breath. Before she could change her mind, she spoke softly. "I forgive you, Stretch."

Big Gust put his large hand on Stretch's shoulder. "You'll need to work and pay back what you stole. We'll have a talk and decide how you can make things up to folks. But for now you come with me. We'll have Christmas first."

Stretch and Big Gust carried the pig to the sleigh. "We'll get your food back soon," the marshal promised Erik.

When Kate last saw Stretch, he was harnessing his horses. He and Big Gust would drive to the home of the tall Swede's sister.

———

"That's why Lutfisk growled at me, isn't it?" asked Kate, as she and Anders and Erik started out again.

Erik flicked the reins, and the horses moved ahead. "What're you talking about?"

"Remember the day I went through the ice? At first I thought Lutfisk was growling at me. But dogs seem to know which people they can trust, don't they? Lutfisk must have been looking at Stretch."

As they drove on, only the jingling of sleigh bells broke the silence.

Then Kate spoke up. "It's Christmas Eve," she said quietly. "We don't have the tree up."

"We don't even have it cut," said Anders. Usually the Nordstroms chopped down a pine on the afternoon of Christmas Eve. Now, as Anders lay in the back of the sleigh, he looked too tired to care.

The team knew they were headed home and set a brisk pace. When the sleigh hit a drift hard, Anders groaned. "Hey, com'on, Erik! That hurts!"

Erik stopped, helped Anders sit up, and pushed more straw under his bad ankle.

When Erik clucked at the horses, Anders spoke again. "You know, we have our pig. And you'll get your food back, Erik. But even if Stretch works to pay them, what about Josie's family? They're still out of meat for winter."

For a time the three were quiet, thinking about Josie's eight brothers and sisters.

"I know!" Anders exclaimed, sounding the best he had all day. "Let's surprise them! Tomorrow we'll see everyone in church. Let's ask each family if they want to give something to Swensons."

Erik agreed. "We can go around the next day, collecting it all."

"And we can see Josie's new kitten," Kate added.

"A kitten?" asked Anders. Even if it was Josie's, he didn't sound too excited.

"A mother cat died, and Josie's been feeding the baby to keep it alive. The kitten's so little Josie doesn't let it go outside. But every now and then it vanishes."

Erik looked at Kate and grinned. "Maybe there's another mystery to solve."

"Maybe." Kate laughed just thinking about it.

The wind was cold now and bit at their cheeks. Kate drew a scarf around her face. In her mind she saw the Windy Hill farmhouse. Mama would set a candle in the window.

"It says we're waiting for the Christ child," she had told them more than once.

But Kate knew that when Mama lit the candle, she also hoped it would draw Papa home.

"It's Christmas Eve," Kate said again. "Papa hasn't come."

The boys were silent, for there was nothing to say.

The sky was orange with the setting sun when Kate saw a small figure on the road far ahead. Closer and closer they came until she knew it was a man. A man walking with his back toward them.

His shoulders were hunched against the cold. His walk was tired, like someone with sore and bleeding feet. But somehow the man looked familiar.

It was Anders who pulled himself up to see and cried, "Papa!"

At the sound of Anders' voice, the man turned.

In the last glow of the sun, Kate saw it was true. "Papa!" she shouted. Into her cry rushed all the gladness that comes after a long wait.

Erik stopped the horses, and Papa reached into the sleigh to hug Anders. Kate jumped down for her hug, and Papa's arm went around her. His beard and lashes were full of ice, his lips cracked from the cold.

When he climbed onto the sleigh, his legs were stiff, but Papa's eyes shone. He was here with them! Home for Christmas!

And when they drove up to the Windy Hill farmhouse, Mama had four candles in the window.

----

The next morning Mama, Papa, Anders, Lars, Tina, and Kate got up at four o'clock. The house was cold, and the sky still dark.

When Erik's family came to give them a ride to church, they brought a large pine tree. Erik carried it into the front room, and the boughs reached to the ceiling.

Then all of them climbed into the sleigh for the early morning Christmas service. Lanterns bobbing, sleigh bells jingling, they headed into the frosty air.

Erik's father drove, and Mama sat beside Papa, unwilling to be parted, even during the trip to church. Papa had bundled her in a heavy robe, but Mama reached out and tucked her mittened hand beneath Papa's big glove.

The moon was still high in the sky when the horses started up the hill near Four Corners. Kate turned around and looked back to see a string of lanterns following them.

Off to the left was another road with lanterns bobbing in the night. At the top of the hill, lights came from straight ahead. And from far across the valley on the right shone still more lanterns.

From four directions they came—lanterns moving slowly toward church, small dots of light shining in the early morning darkness, growing larger.

When Kate and her family entered the darkened church, candles blazed from every window. More candles glimmered from the Christmas trees. And a candle seemed to glow in Kate's heart.

After the service, Erik's family came into the Windy Hill farmhouse for Christmas breads, cookies, and cakes. Then it was time for Kate to give Tina and Papa their presents.

As she sat down at the organ, she felt afraid. *What if I make a mistake? What will everyone think?* With all her heart she wanted to play well.

In that moment she remembered the hidden message. *The Lord is on my side; I will not fear.* Like Mrs. Berglund, Kate asked for help.

Her fingers grew steady. She wasn't scared anymore. Her notes sounded sure and strong.

As Kate played "Children of the Heavenly Father," someone moved to stand beside her. Yet when Kate looked up, it wasn't Tina she saw, but Mama. Mama with tears in her eyes.

Kate smiled at Papa and started the carol she had learned for him. "Silent Night, Holy Night. . . . Sleep in heavenly peace."

Then Kate received the biggest surprise of all. On the second verse Erik began to sing. His voice sounded scared at first, then clear and strong.

One after another, the others joined in. Erik's family. Tina. Lars. Mama and Papa. Then finally, Anders.

It was going to be a good Christmas, after all.

# Acknowledgments

When I was thirteen years old, someone said to me, "Lois, do you have to ask so many questions?"

At the time I was embarrassed. By now I've discovered that curiosity is a necessary part of being a writer. Those who give answers become my cherished friends.

Among these are Gary and Cris Peterson. They didn't know I'd see in their organ more than a piece of furniture. But they do appreciate curiosity, and so, the organ on the cover is theirs.

Alton Jensen and the Grantsburg Historical Society provided information about countless details. Berdella Johnson shared her family stories and her knowledge of Swedish ways. Alice Biederman offered her gift for music and memories of Big Gust at her family's table. Her husband Leon talked of his experience in making skis. Bertha Iverson told about Spirit Lake School and the lanterns of Christmas morning.

Eunice Kanne gave me her research and wisdom as well as her books, *Pieces of the Past* and *Big Gust: Grantsburg's Legendary Giant*. Walter and Ella Johnson knew about barbed wire fences, boots, and canning jars. Helen Tyberg remembered the cold rides and warm bricks of her childhood. Diane Brask described her experiences with tree climbing, animals, and sprained ankles. Mildred Hedlund told about her relative, Big Gust, and her love for his sister. Randy Klawitter reminded me

143

that a young man can learn to walk in the old ways.

Charette Barta, Ron Klug, Carol Johnson, Jerry Foley, Penny Stokes, and Terry White helped with the manuscript. My husband Roy gave his ideas, his understanding of my curiosity, and his love.

And so, a book is never entirely mine. It belongs to all of you who read and to all of you who know and appreciate the past. I thank you!